ROPE LAW

**Center Point
Large Print**

**This Large Print Book carries the
Seal of Approval of N.A.V.H.**

~ LEWIS B. PATTEN ~

ROPE LAW

CENTER POINT PUBLISHING
~ THORNDIKE, MAINE ~

This Center Point Large Print edition
is published in the year 2003 by arrangement with
Golden West Literary Agency.

The text of this Large Print edition is unabridged. In other
aspects, this book may vary from the original edition. Printed in
Thailand. Set in 16-point Times New Roman type by
Bill Coskrey and Gary Socquet.

ISBN 1-58547-246-8

Cataloging-in-Publication data is available from the Library of Congress.

CHAPTER ONE

Under a warm morning sun, the plateau lay like a slumbering giant, stretching from the Colorado River on the south to the White River on the north. East and west, it was just as wide, and towered over the surrounding river valleys by upwards of twenty-five hundred feet.

Sheer cliffs of rimrock guarded its rolling, grassy top. But men, toiling like ants on its ponderous slopes, had constructed trails here and there that looked from a distance like zigzagging, gossamer threads trailing down from the dark spruce fringe above the rim.

And valleys, like gashes clawed into its surface by the talons of some gigantic bird, broke the plateau into points and ridges, for all the world like fingers pointing southward toward the even larger bulk of Grand Mesa.

In one of these valleys a dust cloud rose. And atop the plateau, a man sat his horse amid a group of others, watching the dust and the antlike horsemen that raised it.

Ed Mallory had been sheriff of Plateau County much of his life. He was old now, and tired, and today he was torn between duty, long an integral part of him, and the instincts of a parent, grown strong over the past fifteen years.

There was irony, he found, in being here, the law of Plateau County riding at the head of a lawless mob whose menacing silence proclaimed that their minds were made up, their course decided. They knew Ed was against them, but they didn't care.

Ed stood in the middle, bound by duty to track down this fugitive to the best of his considerable ability, duty bound as well to defend him when he had done so, even to death if necessary. And Ed was afraid it would be necessary.

Fate, he mused, had a way of placing a man in an impossible position where he was damned if he did, damned if he didn't. For Ed Mallory, today's task was extra-hard, because when a man is old and tired, fighting, even a clash of wills, can become an exhausting ordeal; and harder still because the fugitive was someone well known over the years that were past, someone well understood, someone loved almost as a son might be loved.

Was he guilty? Indications pointed to it. The posse thought he was too. They were so sure that they were determined to hang him, when they caught him, from the nearest tree that would support his weight.

Right now there were those among them who were frightened and filled with doubt. There were those whose bloodthirsty determination was bravado. But they were bound together by the adhesive of pride, and not one would give up and leave, for to do so would be to confess weakness.

Ed had tried to talk them out of it. He'd tried, and he'd failed. Now he must face the consequences of his failure.

Tall and gaunt, he sat his saddle like a statue, looking downward at the other half of the posse, which would climb the plateau by another trail farther north. They'd have the fugitive between them then on the mile-wide ridge, and he wouldn't escape unless he was desperate enough to fling himself from the rim. Ed didn't think he was.

The skin of Ed's face was old, yellowed parchment, lined deeply from the years of living that were almost over now. His eyes were chips of pale turquoise, eyes that could be hard and cold as winter ice in a mountain stream, eyes that could soften with kindness and pity over a crying child.

The posse fidgeted, but Ed was still, his right hand dangling loosely at the saddle skirt. One of the posse said irritably, "Damn it, Ed, you give me the creeps. What the hell's goin' on in that head of yours? You figure you can outsmart us an' let him get away?"

Ed's eyes swept the speaker briefly, coldly. He spoke but he didn't dignify the accusation with an answer. He only said patiently, "When the others get halfway up the trail, we'll move. Until then, we'll stay right here."

The man subsided, unsatisfied and grumbling. The others looked at Ed and looked away. They distrusted him because Joe Redenko had been like a son to him, and because they couldn't understand him, but they weren't yet ready to put their distrust to the test.

A man in the posse shaped a cigarette, and at once half a dozen hands groped automatically for shirt pockets and tobacco. But Ed stayed still.

He was thinking that when a man gets old his mind lives in the past. The present is painful and tiring, the future nonexistent. All he has is the past.

But the past was good, when you thought of it, because heartbreak and trouble dimmed with years, and remembered pleasure and happiness became only that much more poignant.

The loves of a man's life were the things that came back most strongly. Love for a woman, love for little children, love for a boy, now grown to a man. Love for Joe Redenko.

Hunky. Waif. A kid that was bony-thin and dirty, who spoke the four-letter words he heard around home with an innocence that proclaimed they were only words to him, words that were heard but that had no meaning other than the voice tones with which they were spoken. Anger, irritation, disgust.

A kid with big eyes in a thin face, with pasty skin and a tendency to duck every time he passed someone.

Ed remembered Joe the way he was now—lean to lankiness, strong-muscled, moody-faced. He remembered Joe's eyes, bewildered no longer, but angry, and most times hard.

He remembered Joe's hair, black and coarse, and the way he used to smooth it down with water before Joe trotted off to school. He recalled the skinned knuckles Joe usually had in those days, the black eyes, the bruised and beaten mouth from his fights in the creek bottom back behind the school.

A voice said, "They're halfway up," in a challenging tone.

Ed looked at the man sourly. "All right. Let's go. Spread out in a line, close enough to see each other but not so far apart that we don't cover every inch of the ground."

Motionless, he watched them move away. They rode in a group, dropping a man off about every two hundred yards. A cold knot of fear began to build in the pit of Ed's stomach.

It wasn't physical fear, or even fear for himself. Age had stolen all that from him long ago. A man as near the end of his life as Ed, who has lived with danger, does not fear death. It was another kind of fear, fear that some trigger-happy member of the posse, scared by Joe Redenko's reputation, would put a bullet into him even after he'd dropped his gun and surrendered.

But there was nothing Ed could do about it. Nothing now. It was out of his hands.

Sometimes, not often, Ed's mind would make a little

wordless prayer. When it did, his eyes would lift involuntarily to the sky. They did so now. Then he touched his heels to the sides of the brown gelding and moved uphill to the crown of the ridge. Here he dropped behind the moving line of men so that he could see the men at both ends.

The men at one end of the line moved down a ravine that was choked with quaking aspen, beat their way through, and emerged again atop the next ridge. The other end moved across rolling sagebrush country. Always Ed's eyes scanned the land ahead.

There was a cabin, he remembered, not far ahead. On the east side of the ridge it was, sod-roofed, sagging, grayed with the years of sun and storm. Maybe Joe would hole up there. Again Ed's eyes lifted briefly to the sky.

But his mind kept drifting into the past, and he asked himself: Where did I fall down? Where did it begin? What makes a kid go bad?

He frowned reflectively as he realized that some part of his mind was doing exactly what the posse had already done—tried Joe and found him guilty, condemned him.

Yet he could also realize that, while Joe might be innocent of this murder, he had long since gone bad in the accepted sense of the term. He had set himself apart from other people, hating them, hated by them.

"And why not?" Ed growled angrily aloud. "Why the hell not? All his life they've been workin' at him, peckin' at him. Who the hell wouldn't turn sour?"

A distant shout rose, faint in the still, clear air. Not a shout from Ed's bunch, but a partly distinguishable shout from someone in the other half of the posse far down the ridge: ". . . . found his horse!"

9

The shout made Ed's bunch turn eager and begin to hurry. Ed touched heels to the gelding's sides and hurried too, keeping his same distance behind the line.

He tried to remember in exactly which draw the cabin was. He'd spent some time in that cabin as a young man, riding for 2-Bar and Old Man Weatherbee. His face softened with his recollections. Wild, they'd been, that crew of Weatherbee's. Wild and shaggy as the wild horses they gathered on the north end of the plateau and drove down this ridge into the corral on the point. Wild enough to rope a deer, wild enough to ride down wolves, even through timber, a man on each side of the wolf and both blazing away at him with a six-shooter.

The wild horses were gone and so were the wolves, but the other game had multiplied until now it was no chore at all to keep a cow camp supplied with fresh game.

That old cabin had been Weatherbee's cow camp. Ed's mind pictured it, and the land that surrounded it.

It sat in a grassy clearing that sloped rather sharply toward the rim, a one-room log cabin with the roof extending out over the dirt in front, its free edge supported by stout roof poles that could support the carcass of a deer, hung there to cool out during the night. Below it, perhaps a hundred yards, a spring seeped out of the draw and ran through a pipe to a series of hollowed-out aspen logs that served as watering troughs for cattle and horses. For fifty yards around the troughs the ground was dusty and bare, marked with the hoofprints of a thousand cattle.

Ed tried to remember how many years it had been since he'd seen that cabin. Maybe it wasn't even there any more. Maybe it wouldn't make the refuge for Joe Redenko that

Ed hoped it would.

Something about the ridge ahead stirred a memory in Ed Mallory. And then he saw a break in the trees, where a trail led down.

The report of a rifle snapped out, muffled by the ridge that lay between it and Ed, but echoing back from the rims across the canyon. Ed's eyes touched his posseman on the far right, who now was skylined atop the ridge. The man was down, scrambling to cover, leaving his horse to stand in the open.

Ed's mouth twisted into a grim smile. It was all right now. His hope had been realized. Joe Redenko was up in the cabin.

CHAPTER TWO

They were waiting for him when he rode up, bold defiance in their faces. Ed knew they'd already talked this over and made their decision.

Ed asked tonelessly, "Well?"

"We'll wait till night. No damn sense lettin' him shoot at us. We'll wait till night an' then come up on the blind uphill side of the cabin. Things are goddamn dry right now. Even them old logs will burn. When it gets hot enough he'll throw down his guns an' come out."

Ed looked at them, one after the other. The bold defiance was still in their eyes but they couldn't meet his glance for long. One after another they shifted their eyes uneasily away. Ed felt a vast contempt.

A mob. A gang with courage enough to take the law into their own hands collectively, without a whit of courage individually. Ed had heard one of them say on the way from town, "Suppose we do lynch the bastard? You think the county's going to try twenty of us for hangin' a killer like Redenko? Two or three men, yes. Twenty, no. Hell, each one of us'd be entitled to a separate trial. The county ain't got enough money for twenty separate trials."

Ed said wearily, "All right. Spread out and find holes for yourselves. Save your ammunition. No sense making this sound like a Fourth of July picnic."

He watched while they scattered. They left their horses below the top of the ridge and went over afoot, slipping from brush clump to brush clump like boys playing at cowboys and Indians.

Ed was tired suddenly, appallingly tired. He'd tried so hard with Joe. But one man can't do it all. He's got to have help. And Ed had had no help.

You try to teach a kid that the world is fair, but how can you make him believe it when he's hurt constantly by its unfairness? You try to teach him that people are essentially good, while everybody in town seems to be seeing just how much like a bastard he can be in his dealings with the boy.

Ed grunted a single, obscene word disgustedly, and rode over the ridgetop. He was straight as a ramrod in his saddle. Without haste, he rode toward the cabin along a direct route, letting the horse choose his own pace.

He saw the blue gleam of a rifle barrel in the cabin window. But he didn't flinch, and he didn't stop. Joe's eyes were good, and Joe wouldn't shoot Ed no matter what.

A posseman, hidden, yelled, "You goddamn fool! Don't trust that lousy hunky!"

Ed rode on. Before the cabin he dismounted. "Don't

come to the door, Joe. They'd risk hitting me to hit you." And he went inside.

It was good to get out of the sun, and it was cool in the cabin. Ed thumbed back his hat and wiped sweat from his bony forehead with the back of one frail hand. He looked at Joe Redenko and grinned, because he could always see the boy in Joe.

There wasn't much boy in Joe any more. His face was scowling, full of bitterness. His body was charged with an electrifying vitality that breathed menace. His eyes were black and hard.

Ed picked up an overturned chopping block and put it on its end. Then he sat down. Joe watched him uneasily.

Finally Ed said, "I'd have come after you alone, but they don't trust me where you're concerned. They came along to see I didn't let you get away."

Joe snorted savagely. "Don't kid me, Ed. I know what they want."

"Yeah. I suppose you do."

Something panicky touched Joe's face. "You ain't goin' to let them do it, are you?"

Ed didn't answer. He just looked at Joe steadily until Joe muttered, "Sorry, Ed."

"It's all right."

"But how the hell you goin' to stop them?" He watched Ed's face, and something went out of his own. "I see now. We die here together, is that it? We let the sons-of-bitches smoke us out and then shoot us down."

"Maybe I'll think of something."

"Yeah. Maybe not, too." Joe fished makings from his pocket and shaped a cigarette with fingers that shook slightly. "You didn't ask whether I'm guilty or not."

"I'm not a judge, son. I'm just the sheriff." He tapped his shirt pocket. "They made me write out a warrant, so I got to bring you in if I can. I don't have to judge you."

Joe opened his mouth as though to speak, but changed his mind. He sat down and lit his cigarette.

Ed could feel the young man's eyes studying him, but he didn't speak, and after a while some of his own calmness seemed to creep over Joe. Joe's hands, holding the cigarette, ceased to tremble. He even managed a tight smile. "It's good to see you, Ed. It's good to have you here." He turned his face away, and his voice was strange. "It's good to have you . . . I mean, thanks for not jumping to conclusions."

"I raised you, Joe. I know you. I don't have to jump to conclusions."

"But I've done . . . a lot of things. Word gets around, and you ain't deaf."

"No saints on earth, boy. We all got things we ain't proud of." He pulled an ancient silver watch from his pocket. "Noon. Full dark at eight. Get some sleep if you need it. I'll watch."

There was a touch of amazement in the young man's eyes. But he didn't argue. He stretched himself out on the rusty springs of the bunk at the back wall and within minutes was snoring softly.

CHAPTER THREE

The hours crept past. Occasionally outside, a man in the posse would yell, "Sheriff! Ed! What the hell's goin' on down there? Goddamnit, why don't you answer?"

Ed didn't move, save for an occasional slight shifting to ease the hardness of the chopping block against his bony buttocks. Silent, a defeated man who could see the end, he stared out the doorway unseeingly. He heard the shouts outside, heard their tone change as the afternoon drew toward its close. There was excitement in the shouts now, and brutal anticipation. They were whipping themselves up to the pitch necessary for a hanging if they caught Joe alive, for shooting him down if they could not.

Ed's mind was going back over the years. For the first time in a long while, he let his mind go back to the beginning.

He remembered Marian, who had been his wife, and something dried and tightened deep in his throat. For their time had been short, so very short. And then she had died, giving birth to Ed's son, who died with her.

Otherwise, Joe Redenko's life might never have become enmeshed with Ed's own.

For a while after Marian's death, Ed tried to still the tortured bitterness of his mind by keeping it drugged with whisky. He quit because he found it didn't work.

Joe Redenko awoke with a start, snatching for his gun. Then he grinned shamefacedly and swung his feet over the edge of the bunk to the floor. The springs protested as he stumbled to his feet. He said, his eyes blank with sudden awakening, "How long did I sleep, Ed?"

"Two-three hours. Feel better?" Ed looked at his face, shining with sweat, at his grimy shirt, now rumpled and stained at armpits and chest.

Joe grunted. "Ain't been awake long enough to tell."

He fumbled in his shirt pocket and drew out a damp sack

of Durham. The papers were dry, so he shook flakes of tobacco into one and made himself a smoke. He offered the sack to Ed, who shook his head, then reconsidered and took it. Joe held a match to Ed's cigarette, then lighted his own. "Found a way out yet?" he asked.

Ed shook his head. Without seeming to, his eyes studied Joe, trying to see the young man clearly and without the prejudicial favor of a man for a son.

God, but the boy had changed! Ed could see it now. The thin, tanned face was the same, its high cheekbones giving it a hollow-cheeked look. The mouth was the same, wide and strong, firm-lipped, except that perhaps the lips were more compressed. In the eyes was the greatest difference. Always somber, always moody, they were bitter now, and colder. Ed wondered how long it had been since Joe had really laughed, how long it had been since he'd really smiled at anyone save Ed himself.

Late afternoon, and the sun hung low above the horizon. Outside, the posse talked back and forth with angry impatience, and finally a single voice shouted, "Ed! Goddamnit, Ed, if you're all right, sing out! Otherwise, we're goin' to treat you just like we treat him."

Ed smiled without humor. "That's Ledbetter. Molly's old man. He hates you the worst of all of them. Mebbe without him I could talk some sense into them. But he'll keep it going."

"I should've killed him before I left town the first time."

Ed shook his head. "You don't kill people for what Ledbetter's done."

Joe laughed harshly. "No. He's never broken a law in his life. He's a big man—a damned big man. He goes to church every Sunday regular as clockwork. The son-of-a-bitchin' hypocrite!"

Ed looked at Joe, his expression still and unreadable. He looked away so that Joe wouldn't see the things in his eyes, pity, compassion, and regret. He said, "Talk it out, Joe. Get it out of your system. You've bottled it all up inside yourself so long that it's poisoned you."

"You're damned right it's poisoned me!" Joe put his forearms down on his knees and stared at the packed-dirt floor. After a while he began to talk.

He'd been little when his folks had brought him to Du Bois. Maybe nine or ten. Small for his age, but tough as wire, and dirty and ragged. His father, big Mike Redenko, had been foreman of a section gang for years, but he'd fallen under a freight and lost an arm. His right arm.

They retired him on a pension so small it scarcely would support him, and he came to Du Bois to live because he figured it would be cheaper than a larger place.

Big Mike was a man who had gloried in his strength. When he lost his good right arm, he figured his strength was gone. He took an escape route that better men have taken, and worse, but in the end he was the same as all the others. Sodden, vicious, brutal. Or unconscious, and that was the way Joe learned to like him best.

Mrs. Redenko, Sonja, tried to hold things together for a long time. She tried to cope with Sam Breen's dunning for something on the grocery bill when there wasn't anything and she knew there never would be. Big Mike took the pension checks and cashed them, and if he made it home with two dollars to last the month he was lucky.

Sonja Redenko was a young woman at thirty, and pretty, too, beneath the lines that worry and hard work had worn into her face. She had a body that was strong and lithe and beautiful. She had a starving for affection that was never satisfied by Mike, who greeted her with blows and curses more often than not.

Sonja found a way out too. But it wasn't an easy way.

Men had always been after Sonja, for as long as she could remember. The first time it was hard to smile back at a man's smile, harder still to make the light conversation that was necessary as a preliminary. The second time was easier, the third easier still.

After that it seldom bothered her, and there was money to pay Sam Breen for the groceries, money for coal in the winter, for Joe's overalls and shoe repairs. Sometimes there was even money for a dress for Sonja.

Joe never quite understood why the family's financial status had changed. At least not then. He only knew there was enough to eat, for once. There were new overalls to wear instead of the old ragged ones. And no longer did his feet stick through the soles of his shoes.

He'd hear them come, never more than one on any particular night, and he'd hear voices briefly before his mother's bedroom door closed. Sometimes the voices were jolly with good humor, but more often than not they were either thick with liquor or thin with furtiveness and haste.

It was lying in his darkened bedroom that he first became familiar with Roscoe Ledbetter's voice, unctuous, hypocritical, and sometimes heavy with passion. At first Ledbetter came once a month, then once every two weeks, then once a week, but it was always on Saturday night, early so that Mike Redenko, staggering home from the saloon, wouldn't find him there.

Joe was tough and able to fight his way out of almost anything. Yet underneath he was frightened and uncertain, and there was no security for his small mind anywhere in the world, least of all at home, where his father beat and cursed him, where his mother, harried by worry and remorse over what she was doing, had less and less thought for him.

But he found a small measure of security in school, in the wonders of the printed word. He read well, progressing with steadily improving skill through the primer, the second reader, the third. By the time he was eleven, he was reading adult books: *A Tale of Two Cities, David Copperfield, The Count of Monte Cristo.*

And also by the time he was eleven, he knew all there was to know about the way his mother earned their living.

He learned that the hard way, going to school one crisp, cool morning in October. Willie Breen, the bucktoothed son of Sam Breen, started it, having heard his father and mother talking about Sonja's strange prosperity the night before when he was supposed to have been asleep. "Yah, Joe Redenko! You ain't so big! Your ma's nothin' but a whore!"

It came unexpectedly and without provocation. It came out of Willie Breen's resentment because Joe had blacked his eye and bloodied his nose the year before in front of Molly Ledbetter. It came out, and then Willie Breen ran, with Joe in pursuit, and because kids are the way they are, pretty soon the whole schoolyard was yelling, "Yah, Joe Redenko! Your ma's a whore! Your ma's a whore!"

Most of them didn't even know what the word meant, except that it was bad.

Erna Hamilton, the teacher, thirtyish and a spinster, came to the schoolhouse door, bell ringing, face flaming. And Joe Redenko ducked into the creek bottom and headed upstream toward the plateau.

At first there was only the hurt, burning like a branding iron against his soul. There was the hurt and the awful humiliation, and then, later, there was the realization that the accusation was true. With a boy's innocence, he had paid little or no attention to Sonja's callers. Nor had he reasoned out her sudden ability to pay the grocery bill at Sam Breen's store.

But now the pieces fitted.

Eleven years old he was, and faced with a problem that few adults could have solved. He traveled until he was exhausted and then he drank from the stream and lay down in a grassy spot of shade.

His soul still shrank when he thought of Willie's words. His mind could not repeat the word Willie had used. He lay in the shade and dreamed of the time when he would be grown, hard and lean and tough. He'd pack a gun low on his hip the way Sheriff Ed Mallory did. People would look at him and whisper their awe. "That's Joe Redenko. Thirty notches on his gun an' he ain't yet twenty. Worse'n Billy the Kid ever was."

No one would dare to say the words Willie Breen had said. Not now.

"I understand he's back in Du Bois looking for Willie Breen. I wouldn't want to be in Willie's shoes."

But through his daydream there persisted the realization

that he wasn't grown and he wasn't a gunman whom everyone feared. He was only a boy.

Tears coursed down his grimy cheeks. His thin body shook with sobs, tortured, terrible sobs. Until exhaustion came, nothing could stem the tide.

He slept, and when he awoke it was dark, and bitter cold.

He was shivering so badly his teeth chattered, even when he clenched them tight. He was hungry, and he was scared. He heard the sounds around him made by the night creatures in their foraging for food. Ahead of him the plateau loomed black and forbidding. Ahead lay unknown terror, and hunger, and cold.

Perhaps a freightyard wisdom deep within him told him that nothing is solved by running away. So Joe retraced his steps, to find that he hadn't even been missed.

He went back to school the next day, and came home that night with his knuckles skinned, with one eye black and one lip swollen and split.

Perhaps it was on that day that hate was born full grown within his heart—hate for the whole human race. Perhaps the hate came more gradually. But its first stirrings, at least, began that day in the sly, whispered comments made by his classmates, in their knowing, leering looks.

It was fed through the succeeding years by injustice and contempt.

Joe Redenko knew what was going on at home. He knew that the town knew. In his boyish way he tried to change it, tried to help. And all he earned for his efforts was one man's undying hatred, which was born of fear and shame.

Roscoe Ledbetter owned the bank. It wasn't a large bank or an imposing one. It was built of yellow sandstone, and inside it was cool and dark and musty. It smelled of dusty leather upholstery, of moldy ledgers and stale cigar smoke.

There was a false partition two thirds of the way across the foyer, in which were two brass-grilled windows. One of these was always closed off by a sign strung on a brass chain: "Next window, please."

Behind the partition sat a number of roll-top desks and chairs, and at the far rear of the room was a monstrous iron safe, standing taller than a tall man, and over six feet wide. On its front were scrollworks surrounding an ornate, garishly painted eagle, which split down the middle when you opened one of the safe doors.

From eight to six on any day, including Saturday, you could find Roscoe Ledbetter sitting at one of the roll-top desks behind the partition like some kind of pagan god, deciding with a brief, cold smile or with a frown and shaking head the financial fate of the applicants that came before him.

Up at the grilled window sat spinster Susan Poole on a tall stool, handling what deposits and withdrawals came in and doing bookwork between times.

A sleepy, dingy business, run with dusty efficiency, cold logic, and no sentiment. No one in the town knew that in the dry heart of Susan Poole burned a desperate kind of longing to be noticed and loved by Roscoe Ledbetter. No one in town suspected that Ledbetter himself had human juices, or that he visited Sonja Redenko nights because his wife, Patience, was afraid of another pregnancy.

But Roscoe knew that if he were discovered, he would be ruined. His wife would leave him, taking their daughter, Molly, with her. The townspeople would snicker at him behind their hands, and would lose confidence in his bank as quickly as though he had been caught gambling.

And yet, beginning on Friday morning, he would start to think of Saturday night, and of Sonja Redenko.

He tried for control. He shamed himself. He swore he would not go to Sonja's house this Saturday night. But always he went. And always he came away satisfied but feeling unclean and unable for a time to look either Patience or Molly directly in the eye.

Ledbetter was a short, balding, muscular man of forty-five. An elder in the town's Methodist church, he hadn't missed a service for more than five years. When the parishioners sang the closing hymn, it was always the deep, strong baritone of Ledbetter that led them. Lately, however, since he'd been seeing Sonja, his voice did not ring out so strongly, as though some of Saturday night's shame had carried over to Sunday morning.

And Ledbetter liked to walk, a rather strange and therefore noticeable preference in this country of horses and horsemen. There were those who had seen him of an evening five miles from town, striding along as though he owned the world. From his walking he derived his physique, of which he was proud, and his darkly tanned complexion of which he was also proud, since it made his graying hair appear distinguished.

A man of conflicting desires and emotions. A man in whom right and goodness warred endlessly with greed and sensualism. A man who would never know peace because greed and sensualism nearly always won, and who therefore was plagued with guilt and a burning need to atone for the times it did.

Church and a search for God were his answer. But, though he went to church every Sunday, he never found God.

So he lived, behind his cold gray eyes and businesslike exterior, with a cancer of guilt upon his soul.

This particular Saturday came and went for Joe Redenko with agonizing slowness. His mind was made up. Saturday was Roscoe Ledbetter's night for visiting his mother, and he intended to stop Ledbetter on the way into the house and ask him to go away—to stay away.

Had he caught Ledbetter going in, as he intended, the whole course of his life might have been changed. Ledbetter, his shame discovered, could have passed off his visit as a business one, could have deliberately misunderstood the boy and gone away, never to return.

But Joe did not catch him going in. Ledbetter, being anxious, came half an hour early, as soon as full dark laid its anonymity upon the town.

Joe heard them talking, and then heard Sonja's door close.

He crawled through his window and went around to the front of the house. His face was burning, and his body was bathed with sweat. He imagined his mother and Ledbetter together, and felt a consuming, helpless fury. He began to tremble, as though from cold, and his determination to speak respectfully to the banker vanished.

Endless hours seemed to pass before he again heard Sonja's door. Shortly thereafter, the front door opened and closed quietly. Suddenly Joe turned cold as ice. His throat closed, and he felt as though he were choking.

Just short of the gate, Ledbetter paused and scanned the

street in both directions.

The Redenko house stood by itself, surrounded by vacant lots. Across the street and halfway down the block stood its nearest neighbor, occupied by Frank Lovejoy, a bachelor, whose interests were academic and who therefore had little notice for the comings and goings of his fellow men.

Apparently satisfied that no one was in sight, Ledbetter stepped through the gate. Then, so abruptly that he started violently, he saw Joe, standing just to one side of the walk.

Joe had opened his mouth to speak, but Ledbetter's instantaneous reaction snapped it shut so savagely that he bit his tongue. Ledbetter's powerful hand shot out, grasped him by the shirt front, and yanked.

Joe released a thin cry of fear, which Ledbetter stifled with a hand clamped over his mouth. "You sneaky little son-of-a-bitch! What're you doing out here? Spying on me?"

Unable to speak because of Ledbetter's stifling hand, and frozen with fear, Joe shook his head dumbly. He began to whimper softly. Ledbetter flung him away in disgust. Then, thinking perhaps that the street would not forever remain empty, he dragged Joe back into the shadows.

"Damn you, say something! Your ma said you were in bed."

Joe struggled manfully with his fear. "You just stay away from her. You quit comin' here. I know what's goin' on."

For an instant there was silence. Then Ledbetter's voice, tight with violence, low pitched too because of his own guilt-ridden fear, said, "You know what I'll do if you say you seen me here? I'll have that floozie you want me to stay away from run out of town. If that happens, your old man's going to find out what's been going on. You know what he'll do? He'll kill her! You want that to happen?"

Joe shook his head vigorously, trembling like a dry leaf in fall.

"Then keep your dirty mouth shut! Understand?"

Joe nodded.

Ledbetter dropped him. Joe crouched on the ground, hating, wanting to kill the man before him, but helpless and without the strength to move. Ledbetter faded away into the darkness, and Joe heard the gate squeak shut.

He was too shocked, too appalled to cry. Shivering, he got up and stumbled around the side of the house to his open window. Without undressing, he flung himself down across the ragged covers of his bed.

"You wait," he whispered. "You just wait till I get big. Goddamnit, I'll make you sorry. You wait an' see."

To Joe's young mind, Ledbetter was the personification of all that was evil, and he hated the man with the bitterest intensity of which he was capable.

Yet had he been older, he would perhaps have detected the note of shame in Ledbetter's voice. He might even have understood it. He might have understood about the way good and evil fights inside a man.

An older Joe Redenko would have known that, basically, Ledbetter was a good man with a strong conscience, or the visits he made to Sonja would not have bothered him so.

Joe might also have known that all of Ledbetter's anger was not caused by the fact that he had been caught and was afraid Joe would tell. Part of it was occasioned by his own conscience and guilt.

Ledbetter would go on hating and fearing Joe. Joe knew

Ledbetter had visited his mother and Joe might talk.

And even if Joe didn't talk, Ledbetter would be reminded of his guilt every time he saw the boy. Joe had become Ledbetter's conscience, unwillingly brought to life.

CHAPTER FOUR

Outside the besieged cabin, the noise was increasing, but it had not reached the pitch of frenzy that would come later. Holding the posse in check was the element of time, and Ed Mallory knew from experience that the men would remain relatively calm unless he and Joe showed themselves, or tried to get away.

Joe sat tense and sweating on the edge of the bunk. The knuckles of his hands were white from the strain of his clenching and unclenching fists.

Ed knew Joe's next memories would be perhaps the most painful of all, and his voice was purposefully calm as he said, "Don't stop, Joe. It'll do you good to get it all out of your system."

Joe looked at Ed in an odd way, his face tense and without color. Automatically he fished for the sack of Durham and built a smoke. He offered the sack to Ed, but Ed shook his head. Frowning now, Joe went on, and his words showed an insight and understanding that only the years could have given him.

Sonja Redenko must have realized from the way Joe was acting that something was wrong. And, being far from dull, she thought she knew what it was.

Yet how do you explain to an eleven-year-old boy something like what Sonja wanted to explain? You don't, and Sonja knew it. There is no explanation, except that you are doing something terribly wrong and that, furthermore, you will go on doing it because once started there can be no turning back.

She began to explain half a dozen times, but before the boy's confused, clear-eyed, embarrassed glance, she became speechless, confused herself. Justify faithlessness and adultery by the pressures that life builds in a person's soul? Explain a hunger for affection that finds its outlet in the arms of strange men who pay for favors? Explain what you have done by a desperate need for money?

Joe would have said, "But ma, I love you. Ain't that enough?" or "Ma, you could've gone to work. An' I could. Between us, we'd of made enough."

Worst of all, she knew he would have been right. There had been no real excuse for what she'd done. She had simply been striking back at life's unfairness and cruelty. She'd let bitterness cloud moral values and good judgment. In the end, she'd hurt Joe.

Too late, she tried to make it up to him with a sudden unaccustomed burst of affection, but it came too suddenly. He was suspicious of it.

Sonja was sorry, desperately so. But she was destined not to be sorry long. Because somehow the knowledge of what was going on found its way into Big Mike's drunken brain.

Perhaps he overheard something in the saloon. Perhaps he figured it out for himself, or perhaps someone deliberately sent him an anonymous note.

Sonja never knew. Long afterward, for a short while, Joe suspected Roscoe Ledbetter, but gradually he became con-

vinced that not even Ledbetter could be so small and con-
niving, so dangerously craven as deliberately to get two
people killed to save himself from discovery.

But Mike found out.

Monday night it was. The Monday following Joe's
encounter with Ledbetter.

Sonja had a caller. Joe was asleep, but he was so tense, so
frightened these days that the slightest sound awakened
him.

The sound that awakened him tonight was the squeak the
front gate made in closing.

He paid it no attention, thinking only that his mother's
caller was leaving. Then, on the heels of the gate's squeak,
he heard the back door opening cautiously.

Still he paid no attention, for his mother often went into
the kitchen late at night, as though vigorously scrubbing
clothes or washing the floor could cleanse her conscience.

Suddenly Joe heard his mother's bedroom door flung
open, and heard his father's enraged bellow. Close on the
heels of that, he heard the confined roar of two shots.

He'd been on his feet, and headed for the door. Now he
stopped, more frightened than he had ever been before,
able to remember but one thing, Roscoe Ledbetter's angry
words: ". . . your old man's going to find out what's been
going on. . . . He'll kill her!"

Frozen with terror, Joe stood utterly still, his hand on the
doorknob. It took the greatest effort he was capable of to
open it and look out.

He saw his father standing in the doorway to his mother's
room, a smoking pistol in his left hand, empty sleeve dangling where his right should have been. As Joe watched, the

29

pistol clattered to the floor.

Like a man in a stupor, Mike Redenko stumbled into the bedroom. Joe advanced until he could see inside. His father was down on his knees beside the prone figure of Sonja Redenko. He was crying, in long, shuddering sobs.

Joe turned and ran. He plunged out into the back yard and took to the brush behind the house.

He ran until he could run no more, but this time he did not head for the plateau. Instead, he ran to the river, and westward along its course until he found an island he could wade to.

On the island, he found a thick clump of willows, and burrowed into them. He had the feeling that if his father found him, he would kill him too.

Hunger brought him out of hiding about noon the following day. And Ed Mallory's posse caught him in the open where there was no cover and no place to hide.

Ed sent the posse on, and got down beside Joe. Ed wasn't so old then. He was a vigorous, dangerous, fearless man, a kind of idol in young Joe's eyes. He didn't mention what had happened, or say where he was headed. He only said, "Lord, you must be hungry. So happens I got some cold meat an' biscuits in a sack behind the saddle. Want 'em?"

Joe nodded, unspeaking. Ed went over and untied the sack, a white muslin one. Joe wolfed down the food and drank from the canteen Ed offered him. All the while, Ed kept watching him thoughtfully.

When Joe was finished, Ed said, "Somebody'll figger out what ought to be done about you. Meantime, how'd you like to stay with me?"

Joe didn't answer.

"Know I'm after Big Mike, don't you?"

Joe nodded.

"You hold that against me?"

A blaze of anger lighted Joe's eyes. "He kilt my ma. Git him. Make him pay fer it."

"All right. You'll stay with me a while?"

Joe nodded.

Ed grinned at him, a little uncertainly. "Good. You go on to my place, then. Know where it is?"

Joe nodded. The Sheriff found a scrap of paper and scribbled a brief note. "I might not be back for a day or two. Meantime, you got to eat. Give this note to Chang Chung, over at the restaurant. He'll feed you till I get back."

Joe wanted to thank him, but the words stuck in his throat, and all he gave Ed was a sullen nod.

Full now, he took his time going back to town. He dawdled around by the river bridge, throwing rocks into the stream and thinking. This way he killed the daylight hours, and after dark he crept to the Sheriff's small house and went in.

He was frightened. He was scared to light a lamp for fear someone would come and accuse him of stealing.

But no one came.

The night was a night of horrible dreams, through which Ledbetter stalked, cursing Joe, and through which Big Mike also stalked, firing a revolver, his face twisted with fury and hate.

Joe Redenko woke up screaming.

He was bathed with sweat. The sheets of the bed were soaked with it. But he was calmed somewhat by the cold gray light of dawn that crept through the grimy windows.

He dressed, but the sun was halfway up the sky before Joe could get up the courage to go out and head for Chang Chung's restaurant.

In midmorning it was deserted except for storekeeper Sam Breen, drinking coffee. Sam stared at Joe curiously.

Joe scowled back, feeling that Breen was, in a way, responsible for his mother's death. Breen was the one whose dunning had driven Sonja Redenko to what she did, ultimately to her death. And, Breen was the father of Willie Breen, whose taunts at school had made life unbearable for Joe.

He sat timidly at the counter and shoved the note across at Chang Chung, who only looked puzzled.

Breen came forward and said blandly, "Want me to read it, Chang?"

"Please. Chang no can read."

Breen took the scrap of paper. He scanned it silently, his eyebrows lifting. "It says to give Joe here whatever he wants to eat. The Sheriff'll pay. It's signed Ed Mallory and it looks all right."

Joe said, "Course it's all right. He give it to me hisself."

Breen said, "Feed him, Chang. Mallory will pay." With a final puzzled glance at Joe, he hurried out.

Joe looked at Chang. "Kin I have anything I want?"

Chang nodded, grinning.

"Then I'll start with a piece of that chocolate cake."

Chang's grin widened, but he gave Joe the cake. Later he gave Joe a piece of lemon pie, after that another piece of chocolate cake.

Wisely, he refused Joe a second piece of lemon pie, and insisted instead that he drink some milk. Refreshed and oddly satisfied, Joe left and went back to the Sheriff's house.

He knew he ought to be in school, but he also knew he wasn't going.

Nervously he prowled the house, looking at the Sheriff's things. He found some dresses packed in a trunk that smelled of perfume and moth balls, and faintly remembered the Sheriff's wife, who had been alive when Joe first came to Du Bois.

But these things held little interest for him so he closed the trunk and went on prowling. And at last he found the Sheriff's guns in the back of a closet.

There was an old revolver and cartridge belt, a scarred rifle, and a double-barreled shotgun.

Joe strapped the loaded revolver and belt around his waist, but it was too big and fell to the floor. He found some string and tied the belt together so it would stay up.

He loaded the rifle and pretended that a posse was after him and that he was holed up here in this house, standing them off.

The game held his interest until midafternoon, when he saw Breen and Ledbetter and a couple of others coming up the walk.

They were talking among themselves and did not bother to knock at the door. They just walked in, confronting Joe with startled expressions because of the rifle in his hands, the enormous revolver tied around his waist.

A couple of them grinned, but Ledbetter took a look at Joe's defiant, frightened expression and said angrily, "You see? Already he's got into the Sheriff's stuff. And guns, too. I tell you, he ought to be sent away. I don't want my girl going to the same school with him."

Breen, still grinning, muttered placatingly, "Roscoe, did you ever see a boy who wasn't interested in guns?"

Opposition made Ledbetter angry. He said, his voice rising, "This one's different. Look at his face. Damn it, I tell you he'll come to a bad end. He'll end up killing somebody."

Joe looked at him, and Ledbetter's glance fell away. But not before Joe had seen the guilt and shame in his eyes. Ledbetter wasn't afraid of Joe's influence on his daughter. He wasn't afraid of the way Joe would turn out, either. He was afraid of what Joe knew. He was trying to banish his conscience.

One of the other men, Wayne Slaughter, the town's Justice of the Peace, said, "Nobody'd take him around here. He ain't stout enough to do much work. Best place for him is over at Denver, in the home. They know how to handle his kind."

His kind! Joe raised the rifle, curled his forefinger tightly around the trigger. His throat was nearly closed with fear. But he managed to say, after one false start, "Nobody's takin' me anywheres. You just wait till Mr. Mallory gits back. He said fer me to stay here, an' I'm stayin'."

The men exchanged glances. Their eyes came to rest on Ledbetter. Ledbetter advanced toward Joe, without meeting his eyes. "Uh-uh, boy. You ain't staying here at all. You're taking the night train to Denver. The Justice here's going along with you."

Ledbetter's face had colored slightly. Now he pulled a small black leather pocketbook from his pants and opened it. He extended a ten-dollar gold piece toward Joe. "Here. Spendin' money till you get settled." Ledbetter tried to smile at him, but it didn't come off.

Spending money, hell! It was conscience money. Even Joe was old enough to know that. He struck the extended hand away and the coin fell to the floor. Ledbetter's face paled. He snatched for the rifle in Joe's other hand.

Joe jumped away, his finger tightening involuntarily on the trigger. The rifle roared, deafening in the small, enclosed space.

Its recoil drove Joe back. He fell sprawling, and the rifle clattered to the floor. A hole in the wall told where the bullet had gone.

Ledbetter's face twisted suddenly with fury and fright. He seized Joe by a skinny arm and yanked him to his feet. Joe uttered a high, thin sound of pain. Ledbetter twisted the arm until it was behind Joe's back. "You see that? The little son-of-a-bitch tried to kill me!"

Slaughter and Breen and the other men were white of face, and their hands were shaking. But Slaughter's mind appeared to be made up. He cleared his throat nervously. "Bring him along, Roscoe. We'll stick him in the jail till night. Hell, looks like you might have been right. He will kill somebody before he's through."

Joe began to cry. He wouldn't get to live with Ed after all. Tears ran down his face and he scrubbed at them savagely with his free hand, which was knotted into a fist.

Joe Redenko, the man, sat on the edge of the rusty bunk and trembled with this bitter memory. He looked at Ed Mallory, not noticing that the land outside was gold in the rays of the setting sun. He asked, "What kid wouldn't have hated him, Ed? Maybe I could halfway figure what was

35

eating him, but it didn't give him an excuse for picking at me. I hadn't done anything."

Ed Mallory said slowly, "People are like that. But I've been thinking. Maybe you'd have got a better shake over at Denver in the home than you got in Du Bois. Maybe I didn't do you no favor, taking you in."

Joe said earnestly, "You're the one person that's not to blame for anything, Ed. If there's any good in me, you put it there."

Ed shook his head. "I didn't help you get the chip off your shoulder. You were touchy as hell about your folks. Maybe that was part of the trouble."

Joe muttered reluctantly, "Maybe. Maybe it was."

Ledbetter's roar suddenly filled the air outside the cabin. "Mallory, this is your last chance! Come out and leave that rotten apple to us or we'll give you the same thing we're going to give him!"

Both Ed and Joe glanced out the partly open door. In the minds of both was the question: How long? How long before they'll fire the cabin and drive us out?

CHAPTER FIVE

Joe's thoughts did not remain in the present for long. A hurt, stricken look came into his eyes, and Ed knew he was remembering the days that followed his brief detention in the jail.

Ed had caught Big Mike that same afternoon. They'd caught up with him, driven him to an island in the river, with deep water on one side and exposed, shallow water on the other.

In a line, the posse splashed through the shallow water, knowing that before they took Mike one or more of them might very well be dead.

But Mike was not a cautious sniper. He knew his time was up, and death now held no terror for him. He almost welcomed it, or at least Ed thought so, judging from the way he came out of the brush thicket roaring like a wounded lion and firing his revolver as fast as he could thumb the hammer back and trigger the shots at his pursuers.

He fell in the river's shallow water, riddled by the bullets of the posse.

If Ed suspected that Mike's shots had all been aimed deliberately high, he never said so. The members of the posse had been excited and frightened, and there was no sense in making them feel bad.

Packing Big Mike's limp, bloody body, the posse came back to town.

Ed was genuinely angry when he found Joe in jail. His first action after releasing the boy was to call on the Justice of the Peace, Wayne Slaughter.

"What the kid did was only what any kid would do in the same situation. Figure out what he's been through, Wayne. Then, by God, you sit down and write out an order giving him over to my custody. Turn me down and I'll take it clear to the Supreme Court if I have to."

"You going to adopt the boy?"

"That's what I was figurin' on."

Slaughter shrugged and reached for paper and pen. "You realize you might be sorry, don't you? That boy's got bad blood. It'll come out before he's through."

Ed snorted an obscenity.

He went back to his office, got Joe, and took him home with him. He heard the boy's screams in the night when dreams woke him up.

In the morning, Ed dug into his own pocket to provide caskets for Mike and Sonja Redenko and to pay for their funeral.

He thought Sonja looked real nice the way Ross Dillon, the coroner, undertaker, and feed-store operator, fixed her up. Her hair was neat and she was dressed in her best.

Mike's casket was closed, for Mike had been shot in the head.

When Ed got back home from making the arrangements, he sat down and tousled Joe's wiry hair. "Up to you whether you go to the funeral or not, son. Might be a good idea to go. Show 'em you're not ashamed. On the other hand, if it'll upset you much, I'd stay away."

Joe looked at him. "I'll go."

Ed gripped his shoulder. Then he went out to the kitchen and fixed their dinner.

Joe didn't eat much. He was scared, and Ed's words of reassurance fell on deaf ears. For the first time, Joe was realizing that he was alone in a hostile world. He had little confidence in Ed's ability to keep him in the face of opposition from so many of the town's influential men.

Ledbetter was the banker, and everyone knew the power of money. Money, or the lack of it, had made Sonja do what she had done. If you followed that a little further, money was at the root of all Joe's troubles. Big Mike had lost his arm working for money. He'd turned to drink because without his arm he felt half a man. Because Mike drank, because there was no money for food, Sonja had turned to selling herself. And Big Mike had killed her for it.

Joe thought of Ledbetter, his face hardening. If you had money, as Ledbetter did, trouble couldn't touch you. Look at Ledbetter, if you didn't believe it.

Joe decided that somehow, some way he'd get money himself. Then he'd come back here and show this lousy town a thing or two.

Ed didn't urge him to finish his dinner. He got up and told Joe to wash and comb his hair. Then together they went out to the stable behind the house and hitched up the Sheriff's buckboard.

There were no women at the funeral, for the sordid story of Sonja's and Mike's deaths had long since made the rounds of the town, finding embellishment with each telling. Nor were there many men, since each of the town's men feared that to attend the funeral would be to admit that he had been one of Sonja's callers.

Ed and Joe filed into the nearly empty church and sat down.

The caskets were plain pine, painted black. They lay side by side on a low table draped with a black cloth that dropped to the floor. A bunch of wild flowers in a cheap vase was the only decoration.

Ed flushed and turned to Joe. "Boy, I plumb forgot flowers. But somebody didn't."

Joe didn't answer. He was looking at the two caskets and trembling inwardly. He didn't want to look at his mother in death, but he knew he'd have to.

He had a hysterical desire to laugh. He put his face down into his hands and felt it twist up, not into a laugh, but into a tortured weeping. His shoulders shook.

Striving desperately for control, he lifted his head and looked around. He saw Frank Lovejoy, the bachelor neighbor of the Redenkos', who had known and liked Sonja and who didn't give a damn what anyone thought. He saw Erna Hamilton, dressed in prim black and wearing a veil, come into the church, her back defiantly straight, her eyes sparkling defiance even behind the veil. She was obviously aware that her coming would be frowned upon. But for once in her prim life she had the courage to do what she knew was right.

After what seemed forever to Joe, the minister, Richard Thompson, came from a door at the front of the church and went over to stand behind a high desk upon which lay an open Bible.

His words were unctuous and measured as he read passages about sin and wickedness and retribution. He made numerous references to Mary Magdalene, which went over Joe's head but apparently not over Ed's, for the Sheriff's face flushed with anger. At last the preacher ended on the hopeful thought: "He that believeth in me, though he were dead, yet shall he live: And whosoever liveth and believeth in me shall never die."

He nodded at Ed, and Ed got to his feet, taking Joe's arm. Ed led him up to the casket that was open. Joe could just see inside.

His mother lay there, pale, sleeping, looking as she had looked a hundred times when Joe had risen early and gone into her room to wake her, except that she was fully dressed instead of in her old faded flannel nightgown.

Then Ed Mallory was pulling him gently away. Erna Hamilton, behind him, looked hastily into the casket, looked away, and hurried with rustling skirts from the church.

Only Frank Lovejoy smiled as he looked at Sonja. Joe thought he heard Lovejoy say, "You're happy now, aren't you, ma'am?"

Then he was out in the dazzling sunlight, walking beside Ed and trying not to notice the curious eyes of the townspeople fixed upon him.

They climbed into the Sheriff's buckboard and waited, and after a while the black hearse pulled around from the back of the church, drawn by its team of black horses. Sheriff Ed fell in behind, and the minister drew in behind Ed's buckboard. The procession went along Plateau Street to its far end, which petered out into a horse trail leading up steeply toward the plateau, and turned into the brown, weed-grown cemetery.

Two graves had been hacked out of the dry ground. Rope slings were rigged over each for lowering the caskets.

Again now the minister said a short prayer, and the coroner's men lowered the caskets one by one into the ground.

Joe stood white-faced, watching. This was final. This was the end. His thin hand went out, groping, and took Ed's strong one. Ed gripped the boy's hand. And suddenly the tears that had hung so long just behind the boy's eyelids burst forth.

His body twitched. He dropped to the ground, put his face into his hands, and sobbed as he had never sobbed before.

How long it lasted he never knew. It seemed he had wept for hours, for he was almost completely exhausted when he was through.

Sniffling, he looked around. The graves had been filled

in. Everyone was gone save for him and Ed Mallory. Ed gave him a grin that was kind of sick and said, "What you need now, Joe, is about ten hours' sleep. It ain't going to be so bad, boy. You and me are going to be real friends."

A week ago Joe would have been the happiest boy in town to hear that from Ed. Today he simply did not believe it. Too many things had happened. He was sure that nothing would ever turn out right again.

But the day following his parents' funeral, as he scuffed from school toward the creek bottom to eat his solitary lunch at noon, Molly Ledbetter fell in shyly beside him.

"Joe, I'm sorry about your folks."

He glared at her. Her eyes widened with fright, but she stood her ground, and held his glance with hers. At last Joe said sourly, "Thanks."

"Can I eat my lunch with you?"

"Nothin' stoppin' you, I guess."

He strode away toward the creek. Molly Ledbetter followed a couple of paces behind him.

In the shade of the creek's trees, they sat down, and Joe tore open his lunch. Two sandwiches and a green apple. He ate in moody silence.

Only once did Molly break that silence. She asked, "Did you see my flowers, Joe?"

"What flowers?"

"At the funeral. I picked them for your mother."

Joe looked at her suspiciously. "What'd you do that for?"

Molly flushed. "I don't know. They were pretty. I felt sorry for you, losing your mother. I know how I'd have felt if I'd lost mine."

Joe was silent, munching on a sandwich. At last Molly

asked, "You mad at me, Joe?"

"Mad? Why the hell should I be mad? I don't care what you do. Pick all the damned flowers you want. Do what you want with 'em. Only let me alone, will you?"

He got up then, throwing what was left of his lunch into the creek. He could hardly swallow that last bite, what with the way his throat was closed up. He ran, so Molly wouldn't see that he was starting to blubber.

He found himself a place where he could be alone. And the only way he could stop himself from crying was by thinking of Ledbetter, and hating him.

In the following months hate came to be a habit with him. Hating Ledbetter, he became silent and bitter. Molly tried again and again to be nice to him, but he'd have none of it. She was Ledbetter's daughter.

And then spring came, and school was out. The rest of the kids went fishing or hung around town doing all the things kids do in summer, but Joe went to work at Sam Breen's store along with Willie Breen.

He was twelve that year. Twelve, and shooting up so fast that his jeans hit him four inches above his shoe tops before he could wear them out. Twelve, and building muscles handling barrels of flour and molasses and cases of canned goods in Sam Breen's store.

Ed got him the job. He came home in midafternoon about a week after school was out and asked Joe abruptly, "You want a job this summer, Joe? Sam Breen said he was lookin' for someone."

Looking for someone, hell! Ed had asked Sam to give Joe a job. Maybe Sam owed Ed a favor and couldn't refuse.

But Joe did want a job and knew he'd never get one on

his own. So he went down to Sam Breen's store that same afternoon and said, "Ed said you was lookin' for someone to work for you."

"Sure am, Joe." Breen tried to put on a show of heartiness but he failed to conceal his doubt. "Be hard work, though. Maybe it's too hard for a kid that's as skinny as you."

"I can handle it, I reckon. You try me an' see."

"Suit yourself." Breen shrugged. "Fifty cents a day, seven in the morning till six at night, Saturdays included. Same as I'm payin' my own boy, Willie."

Fifty cents a day. It seemed like a fortune to Joe, who had hardly had a dime in his life to call his own. Fifty cents! He could buy his own clothes now. He could buy some of the candy Breen sold, and for which his body had an insatiable craving. He could save up for a pair of cowboy boots.

Breen put him in the back room first, moving stuff around and unpacking cases. It was hot and dusty, and before an hour was past, Joe was exhausted.

At five-thirty, a wagon pulled up at the dock in back, and Joe started to unload it. Six came, and six-thirty. Breen and Willie went to supper and the front doors were locked, but still Joe worked, carrying in the wagonload of supplies.

At seven-thirty he was finished, and at seven-thirty Sam Breen was back to lock up as though he couldn't quite trust Joe to do it.

Joe dragged himself home, but when he got there he was too tired to eat. He went in and lay down fully dressed upon the bed and instantly was asleep.

The days afterward became a nightmare of exhaustion. But he stood them and he never even thought of giving up.

Gradually, as his body became used to the work, muscles

began to form in his scrawny shoulders and arms and the work became less exhausting.

Joe in the back room, Willie up front, waiting on the trade. Joe didn't resent it. He figured that was Willie's right, since his old man owned the store. Besides, it kept Joe from meeting the townspeople, who never forgot and never let him forget whose kid he was, and what had happened to his parents.

A month. Two. August, and the land lay baking under a merciless glaring sun. Dust in the street, the lawns burned and brown.

Willie, always disliking Joe, now assumed the attitude of boss whenever his father left the store. He gave orders, unnecessary ones sometimes, just for the pleasure of seeing Joe obey.

Joe hated it, but he was under no delusions. He knew that to refuse Willie's senseless orders would be the same thing eventually as giving up the job. He knew Willie, who could be vindictive and sly, who would lie if necessary to achieve his ends.

So he scowled and did what Willie told him to.

Twelve, and every once in a while it seemed that Molly Ledbetter would be near the store at quitting time. Because they lived in the same direction, she often would smile and speak, and then walk along with him as he trudged toward home. Several times he noticed Willie watching them as they went up the dusty street together.

Molly was a lanky girl with dark hair in braids. At the end of each braid there was invariably a small piece of ribbon tied in a bow. Her clothes were nice and clean, and she smelled good. Her eyes told Joe that she thought he was wonderful, and would sometimes sparkle angrily at the cold stares she and Joe got from the townspeople.

Then the chalked hearts began to appear on fences and the sides of buildings; the hearts with the initials ML and JR scrawled inside them. Hearts at first, then words like "Molly loves Joe," or "Joe loves Molly." Finally the obscenities began to appear.

Joe was furious the first time he saw one of them. But he pretended not to notice because of Molly, and came back in the night with a bucket of water and a rag to wash it away.

He was scrubbing out the last letter when he heard a soft, threatening voice behind him. "You little bastard, I figured it was you. I figured you'd come back and write some more of your filth. But why wash that out? Wasn't it dirty enough?"

Joe swung around and saw the blocky, muscular shape of Ledbetter standing there in the darkness. Joe said, heart pounding, "I never either—"

"Damn you, don't talk back to me!" Ledbetter's voice had risen, though it probably could not have been heard twenty-five feet away.

Joe said, "But—"

Ledbetter didn't give him a chance to finish. He let Joe have a vicious, backhanded slap across the face.

There was force in the blow, and Joe hadn't much weight. He fell back, striking the fence with his shoulder blades so hard that it creaked. He slid to the ground, dazed as much by the unexpectedness of the blow as by its force.

Ledbetter hauled him to his feet with a hand entangled in his shirt front. Then he began to slap Joe's face, back and forth, back and forth. The impact of his hand sounded like a beaver tail on still pond water.

Joe struggled, but he was helpless in Ledbetter's powerful grasp. Suddenly Ledbetter let him go. Joe slumped to the ground, his head ringing, his cheeks on fire.

Ledbetter's voice was a tight, savage whisper: "You little bastard, if I catch you writing on fences again, I'll beat your stupid hunky head in. And you stay away from Molly, hear? If I see her with you again, you'll think tonight was easy." Ledbetter was panting from exertion and fury. And then he was gone.

Wild with fury, Joe got up and ran in the direction Ledbetter had taken. He didn't know what he meant to do. He only knew that Ledbetter had to be told the truth and made to recognize it. He had to listen while Joe told him he'd had nothing to do with the writing on the fence.

Oddly enough, Ledbetter was not headed toward home. Joe caught sight of him half a block away and slowed to a walk so he'd have breath to talk when he caught up.

Ledbetter stopped. He stood across the street from Joe's old house, staring at it. Joe approached, silently and cautiously.

There was not much light. Just a little from a crescent moon and the stars. But there was enough so that when Joe came near he could see Ledbetter's face.

There was pain in it, and a kind of haunted loneliness. Joe slipped behind the trunk of a cottonwood and watched from its shadow. Ledbetter was talking, and that was odd, because there was nobody with him to talk to. He said, "I was a fool—a damned stupid fool. I know it now. But it's too late, isn't it, Sonja? It's too damned late!"

Joe felt a chill run along his spine. To hell with talking to

Ledbetter. Ledbetter was nuts. Joe turned and went toward home.

He told Ed he'd had a fight with one of the kids, and Ed let it go at that. Joe's fights were common enough.

But, looking at Joe's disturbed expression, Ed didn't really believe it had been only a fight. It had been more than that, much more.

Trouble was, Ed couldn't get close to Joe any more. The chip on Joe's shoulder was keeping even Ed away.

CHAPTER SIX

Molly tried to walk home with Joe twice after that. Both times he snarled at her so savagely that her face turned pale. But his snarling achieved the desired result. She stopped happening to be nearby when Breen's store closed. She stopped bothering him, though several times he caught her watching him covertly.

Shame chewed at Joe every time he saw her. Shame because he had acceded to Ledbetter's demands through fear.

But the shame couldn't stop the fear. Every time he thought of Ledbetter, every time he saw the man, his face would tighten and twitch where Ledbetter's hand had smashed it.

Fall came, and school began. Both Willie Breen and Molly Ledbetter went back to school, but Joe continued working at Breen's store. He was up front now, part of the time, waiting on trade.

Winter passed, more or less uneventfully. Joe was a hard, steady worker, and Breen's doubt and suspicion gradually changed to approval. And Joe basked in it, because it was something entirely new in his experience.

He knew now the satisfaction, the soul-deep joy to be found in a job well done. He began to feel important, for the first time in his life. He took the trouble to learn each item in the store, and its price. When an item was running low, he made a note of it, so that Breen could order more from the wholesale house in Denver.

Understandably, perhaps, Breen took advantage of his efficiency. He stretched his lunch hour to two and sometimes three hours. He began to come in at eight or eight-thirty in the morning, and to leave around four-thirty.

Joe was flattered at being so well trusted. But his biggest thrill came on the day Breen raised his pay. Breen came in late, as usual, looked around with sudden surprise as though noticing the change for the first time, and said, "Joe, this place looks better than it ever has before."

"Thanks, Mr. Breen."

"I wish Willie would work at it the way you do."

Joe said generously, "It makes a difference when your pa owns the store." But he was flushed with pride.

"Joe, starting Saturday, you get more money. Five dollars a week instead of fifty cents a day."

For a moment Joe couldn't speak. When he could, he said, "You don't have to do that. I—"

Breen interrupted. "I want to. You've earned it."

Breen left at noon, feeling good inside, proud of himself for his generosity to Joe, pleased at the grateful way Joe had behaved.

Willie was home from school with a cold that day, and Breen could see the sullenness and anger coming over

Willie's face as he told his wife about Joe and Joe's raise. When Breen had finished, Willie said sourly, "All I got to say is, you better watch the till with that hunky around."

"Willie!" This from his mother, who disapproved of his utterance of the suspicion rather than of his having it. She'd been doubtful of Joe all along.

And, Breen, hating himself for doing it, couldn't help wondering if he were being wise in leaving Joe alone in the store so much.

Breen knew the temptation that can beset a man at times. Even his wife didn't know how he came by the money with which he'd started the store. He'd told her he inherited it from his grandmother.

But he hadn't. He'd embezzled it. And he'd got away, losing himself afterward in the vast, unpoliced distances of the West.

The amount hadn't been overly large, so they'd stopped looking for him after a while. But even now, when a friend laid a hand on Breen's shoulder unexpectedly, he'd start guiltily, and laugh with nervous relief when he saw who it was.

Breen went back to the store. In the succeeding days he tried to go on as he had been doing, yet in spite of himself he came to work earlier and left later. He cut his lunchtime to an hour.

If Joe noticed the change in Breen's habits, he didn't comment on it. The raise seemed to have spurred him to even greater effort. And gradually the suspicions planted by Willie in Breen's mind began to fade.

Then school was out again and Willie came back to work at the store.

From the first, his coming meant conflict, turmoil, and confusion. He deliberately undid the things Joe did. He blamed his mistakes on Joe. And he began to filch money from the cash drawer, in the hope that Joe would be blamed.

The shortages did not go unnoticed by Breen. Nor did the fact that they'd started after Willie's return escape him.

But his attitude toward Joe began to change. He'd catch himself hoping, almost praying that it was Joe who was stealing from him, and not Willie. He began to dislike Joe, because somewhere deep within himself he suspected that the thief was not Joe, but Willie.

He watched Joe carefully, and studiously avoided watching Willie.

Willie could not, of course, fail to notice his father's changed attitude toward Joe, or the way his father watched Joe. But Willie knew that Breen would never catch Joe stealing. Joe was too proud of his job, too busy working, too well satisfied with his pay. So Willie was forced to take a hand.

It was easier for him than he thought it would be. He waited until his father had gone to lunch one day, leaving him to watch things along with Joe. Then he sent Joe into the back room for something, and while Joe was gone he filched three double eagles, sixty dollars, from the drawer and dropped them into the pocket of Joe's jacket, which was hanging on a coat tree near the door.

When his father came back, he said, "Pa, I ain't real sure of this, but I reckon you ought to know."

"Know what?"

"Well, I hate to say anything. Maybe I'd better not."

"Maybe you'd better now you've started."

Willie's reluctance suddenly vanished. "Well, Joe was actin' funny a few minutes ago when I came from the back room. He was over by his jacket there and he jumped like I'd caught him at somethin'."

Breen stared at Willie closely. Willie looked away. Breen went over and slipped his hand into Joe's jacket pocket. His eyes widened as his hand came out, holding the three double eagles. He muttered thoughtfully, "That's a hell of a lot. There's never been more'n a couple of dollars missin' before."

Willie said quickly, "Maybe he's figurin' on running away. Or maybe he's just gettin' brave because he hasn't been caught before."

Breen nodded. He didn't look at Willie because some hidden part of him was afraid of what he'd see if he did. Instead, he began to think of Joe. He let his anger build up, and piled fuel on it and felt relieved when it leaped higher. Hell, he'd given Joe a job. He'd raised his pay. And this was the way the damned little hunky repaid him!

He thought about Joe's folks. What could you expect, anyway, from a kid whose mother had been a prostitute, whose father had been a sodden, savage drunk?

The more Breen thought about it, the easier it became to convince himself that Joe was guilty. He let his anger rise unchecked.

Thoroughly enraged, he sent Willie to fetch Joe, still without looking at him. Willie stayed in the back room, but Breen knew he was listening. He could almost picture the grin on Willie's face.

Breen held out his hand. In his palm lay the three double eagles. "How long you been sticking your hand into the till?"

Joe's face went white, then flushed with anger. "I never—"

Breen said, "Don't lie about it, for God's sake! I've been missing money for a long time. Willie says he caught you over by your jacket today. He said you looked like you'd been caught at something. I found these in your jacket. They were in the cash drawer this morning."

Joe looked dazed and puzzled, which expressions Breen was more than willing to mistake for guilt. Breen asked harshly, "You figure you can explain where you got sixty dollars?"

"I got more'n that at home. I been savin'."

"Yeah. I'll bet you have got more at home. My money that you've taken out of the till. Well, by God, you're fired. And I'm going to take you down to Ed Mallory an' let him know what you done."

Joe didn't struggle. He went along beside the white-faced, angry storekeeper in silence. Willie stayed behind to watch the store.

The walk to the Sheriff's office seemed to take forever. But at last they were inside, and Joe was looking at Ed's startled face.

Deep within him an awful fear began to grow. What if Ed believed he had done it?

Breen said furiously, "Ed, I hope to God you're satisfied. I took this damned kid because you begged me to, and look what happened. Just what I was afraid would happen. He turned into a lousy thief."

Ed's eyes flashed. He took his feet off the desk and got up. His voice was dangerously soft. "Breen, don't use that tone on me, or that word on the boy, unless you've got iron-clad proof. Unless you saw him do it. Did you?"

Joe released a long-held breath.

"Same as, by God. Willie seen him hangin' around his jacket. Joe jumped like a cat caught in the cream. When Willie told me, I looked in Joe's pocket, and this here's what I found."

"Maybe it's his. He's got a passel of money saved up."

"It ain't his. It's mine. I been missin' money for a long time. I been tryin' to catch this damned kid."

"How long you been missin' money?"

"Months."

"How many months? Ever since Joe's been workin' for you?"

Breen's eyes flashed angrily. "How the hell should I know? Probably ever since the kid came to work for me. Or maybe he just waited till I began to trust him."

Ed looked at Joe. "What about it, Joe?"

Joe squared his shoulders and looked Ed straight in the eye. "I never stole a penny, I never saw that sixty dollars before. Someone must have put it there." Somehow or other, even though he wanted to, he couldn't accuse Willie.

Breen snorted unbelievingly. Ed said, "Breen, I believe Joe. But I see you don't. All right. What do you want me to do?"

For the first time Breen seemed uncertain. Then he scowled determinedly. "Well, first of all, the kid's fired. I don't want him around no more. Besides that, I want all the money he's got saved. It's mine. He stole it from me."

Joe's anger stirred for the first time. "You ain't gonna get a penny," he said defiantly. "That's my money. I saved it. I worked for it. I never stole nothin'."

Breen's face flushed. "By God, I get it or I sign a complaint. I'll see that kid in jail before I'll let this slide."

Ed swore disgustedly. Then he said, "Go on back to the store, Breen. Let me talk to Joe."

Joe held his tongue until Breen was gone. Then he turned furiously to Ed. "You believe him! You think I did it!"

Ed shook his head. "Nope. I don't."

"Then why didn't you tell him to go to hell?"

Ed looked faintly ashamed. "What would you rather do, Joe, give him your money and have this thing dropped, or let him sign a complaint and have it dragged through Slaughter's court? Supposing there ain't enough proof to convict you? Do you reckon that'll make any difference to the people in this town? They been waiting for you to make a slip. Even if Slaughter turns you loose, you'll be guilty in the minds of the townspeople, because your name's Joe Redenko."

Joe stared at him unbelievingly.

Ed's shame seemed to increase. "Kid, I'll stand by you till hell freezes over, if you want it that way. Or, if you give Breen the money, I'll see to it that he keeps his damned mouth shut about it."

Joe seemed to mature in the next few moments. He stopped being a boy and became a disillusioned man. He said, with surly bad temper, "Either way, I'm finished. That's what you're trying to say, ain't it? When I go to look for another job, they'll want to know why Breen fired me. And if I go to trial, it's even worse."

"I hate to admit it, Joe, but you've got it about right."

Joe sat down, tall for twelve, and older than he had been

a few moments before. He stared moodily at the floor for a long time. "What am I goin' to do, Ed?"

Ed's eyes were bitter. "You're goin' to take it, Joe. Life ain't always fair, but sometimes it's more than fair. We got to take it as it comes. Give Breen the money for now, and just keep quiet. I'm goin' to find out who put that money in your jacket. I'll find out who's really been robbing Breen's till."

Joe's eyes told Ed he didn't believe him. He said, "You don't have to look far. Willie's the one that pointed the finger at me. He's got to be the one that put the money there. But even if you know it, how can you prove it?"

"That's the rub. Maybe I can't. Maybe I'll never be able to. But that don't mean I won't try."

"Meanwhile, what do I do?" There was a tone in Joe's voice that Ed didn't like.

"Sit tight. I'll talk to Buss Weatherbee. I used to work for his old man years back. Buss'll give you a job."

Joe got up, white-faced. "To hell with that. I'll get my own jobs from here on out."

Ed Mallory shrugged. "Suit yourself." He watched the boy stalk out, watched the defiant way his head lifted once he reached the street. Ed felt inadequate, helpless. He wanted to ease the hurt in Joe, but he knew that right now he couldn't. Maybe later, when the hurt wasn't so sharp, he'd be able to talk to Joe.

Outside the cabin, the clouds were deepening into purples and grays.

Joe stared across the dirty cabin at Ed. "I should've listened to you, Ed. But damn it, I never touched a lousy penny of Breen's money, and it hurt to be blamed for it!"

Ed nodded. His hand gestured toward the door. "Breen knows it wasn't you. I think he knew at the time. That's probably why he backed down on taking your savings."

"Why didn't he say something, then? Why didn't he give me my job back?"

Ed smiled tiredly. "It's no excuse, but I guess it does something to a man to know his son's been stealing from him, that his own son would steal and then shove the blame off onto someone else. Breen was so busy trying to find reasons why Willie done it, and trying to excuse him, that he forgot how you might be feeling. There always was hard feeling between you and Willie. Breen probably got to figuring Willie'd be all right except for you."

Joe stared at Ed bitterly. "Sure. Try hard enough and you can find an excuse for every one of those bastards out there. But how about me? You going to keep on excusing them even while they put a rope around my neck?"

Ed didn't answer, because there was no good answer he could make. Joe wasn't good at turning the other cheek. Ed guessed nobody really was. Turning the other cheek was a philosophy people preached at the other fellow but never really accepted for themselves.

CHAPTER SEVEN

Joe's memories were racing now, as though to beat the deepening darkness around the cabin.

After Breen fired him, there wasn't much he could do. He'd quit school to work in Breen's store, and pride wouldn't let him go back.

Deprived of the sense of accomplishment and well-being he'd worked so hard and well for in the store, and grown bitter, too, he drifted around town, and inevitably he took up with the loafers and drunks that congregated at the town's single saloon and pool hall. Also inevitably, he met Jake Dalhart, who operated one of the biggest ranches in Plateau County, mostly from a chair by the front window of the saloon.

Dalhart was a short, slender man with balding black hair. Everyone knew about his wife and wondered at their union, for they were as different as the seasons.

Perhaps Dalhart's character was shaped in part by his wife. Quite possibly he was the way he was in defiance of her piousness and narrow-minded self-righteousness. Jessie Dalhart made no bones about the fact that she considered all pleasures of the flesh sinful, whether they were simple pleasures such as dancing and card playing, or the stronger pleasures Dalhart favored. She gave him nothing as a wife that he could not have received from a housekeeper, and the only time he had tried to arouse her she had looked at him with such unutterable disgust that he hadn't tried again.

Thereafter, to Jake, a woman became a challenge, be she the daughter of a hired man or the wife of a friend. The more unassailable she appeared, the greater the challenge she presented.

And the years had taught him that few women could long withstand the siege he could lay to their virtue's citadels when he was determined enough. Consequently, he appeared to hold all women in thinly veiled contempt, though Ed suspected his often-stated beliefs were not necessarily his true beliefs. Ed suspected that Dalhart doubted his own virility. He had failed miserably to stir response in his wife, and therefore felt impelled to prove himself with every woman he met, to destroy her character as a means of bolstering his own.

But Jake's interest in Joe puzzled Ed. He figured it must be a kind of fatherly interest at first, yet if it was, it was a twisted kind. For Jake tried to shape Joe as no father would ever shape a son.

It began when Jake saw Joe in the poolroom in back of the saloon proper one day and wandered back.

Joe was shooting, and doing fairly well, considering how little experience he'd had with the game. Jake said, "Shoot you a game for the beer, kid."

Joe looked up. "All right."

Dalhart let him win and bought the beer. He let Joe win two more and bought two more beers. By that time Joe's eyes were dazed-looking and he was slightly unsteady on his feet.

Right then, Willie Breen came in with an empty pail to be filled with beer for his father. Dalhart said, "I've heard the talk, kid. Everybody in town knows that son-of-a-bitch there is behind your getting canned from Breen's store. Why don't you go on up front and kick the hell out of him?"

Joe knew he could. He'd done it before. But he didn't like to be pushed and he didn't like the look in Dalhart's eyes. He shook his head.

Dalhart said, "What the hell? It's nothin' to me. But come on up front anyway. I'll buy you a beer."

Joe didn't want another one, but Dalhart was friendly, so he went along and stood beside him at the bar while the bartender filled Willie's bucket. As Willie went past on the way out, Dalhart deliberately stuck out a foot and tripped him.

The beer pail hit the floor and the beer splashed up, drenching Willie's front. Willie hit the floor on top of it. He got up madder than a chicken that has fallen into a pond.

He looked at Joe and looked no farther. He sailed in without waiting to ask questions.

His first blow took Joe squarely in the mouth, split his lip, and sent a trickle of blood across his chin. And of course, since he'd done nothing to Willie, it angered him.

Savagely, with single-minded purpose, he fought back. Willie never got a chance to strike another solid blow, for Joe kept him backing across the saloon floor until his shoulders touched the far wall.

Rafferty broke it up. "Come on now, you damn little squirts! What the hell do you think you are, growed-up men? Git out of here, Willie, and tell your pa to come after his own beer. Redenko, you git the hell out an' stay out! I had enough trouble with your old man and I ain't gonna have it all over again with you."

Joe glared at him and started to shuffle away, but Dalhart caught his arm. "Joe's with me, Rafferty. Let him alone. He's a good kid and I like the way he handles himself."

Panting, Joe stood at the bar with Dalhart, feeling good, feeling big and, for once, accepted. Dalhart put himself out to be his most engaging self. "How'd you like to go to work for me, Joe?"

"You mean it?"

"Hell, yes, I mean it. I like you. I like the look you get in your eyes when you fight. You don't have to take anything off the bastards in this town, Joe. Not the way you fight."

So Joe went to work for Jake Dalhart. At first, Jake was a hero to him. Jake, for all his money and the size of his ranch, would work as hard as any of his men. He could ride the meanest broncs in his corral, and did. He could put in the longest hours on roundup of any man and still be good for a night's drinking at Rafferty's.

And Jake seemed to take a personal interest in Joe. He taught him all the intricate, dirty tactics of barroom fighting. He taught him how to throw a knife. He and Joe burned up box after box of .44 ammunition shooting at tin cans stuck up on the corral fence five miles from the town and out in back of Jake's ranchhouse.

Joe never thought, in his gratitude, to ask why Jake was doing all this. It was enough that he was.

But Ed Mallory asked, and he wasn't satisfied a bit with the answer: "Hell, Ed, I like the kid, that's all. He'll make a top hand for me one of these days. But he's green, and besides, every kid ought to know how to take care of himself."

Ed said, "You wouldn't be trying to prove anything, would you, Jake?"

"Prove? What have I got to prove?"

Ed had shrugged, not knowing how to put his vague suspicions into words. But he knew Dalhart, knew how bothered Dalhart was with uncertainty and how desperately he tried to cover it. It seemed to Ed that somehow Dalhart thought of Joe as a son, and was trying to build Joe into the kind of man he wished he himself might be.

Strange and twisted suspicions, Ed told himself firmly, with no foundation to set them on. Too vague to base accusations upon.

So Ed sat back and watched uneasily, wishing he could stop the things Dalhart was doing to Joe, but knowing he couldn't, not without driving Joe away from himself.

Winter came and passed, and summer, and winter again. Joe no longer looked like a boy, but, at fourteen, very much like the man he was soon to become.

He had a gun, which he seldom carried. But Ed knew he used it almost as well as Ed used his own.

No longer did Joe have to fight the other kids his age, or even the older ones. They stayed clear of him, knowing that to taunt him was to court a savage beating.

And Joe was becoming a top hand on Dalhart's D Diamond ranch.

Fourteen. Then fifteen. Then sixteen.

With anyone but Joe, the town would have given credit. Joe was a hard worker. In spite of Dalhart's prodding, he never drank more than a glass or two of beer, because he didn't like the effect it had on him. He was steady and reliable.

But the town had its memories of Big Mike and of Sonja Redenko. The town had its memory of Joe being fired from Sam Breen's store just at a time when Breen was bragging all over town about what a good kid he had working for him. The town figured it out, with maybe a grin or leer from Willie occasionally to aid them. The town guessed that Joe had been caught stealing.

Ed Mallory suspected that Breen had cleared Joe in his mind long ago. Somehow, Breen must have discovered that his son was the guilty one. Ed asked Breen about it one day, and the tipoff for him was the angry way Breen immediately took it up.

"Damn it, Ed, that's over and done with! I'm not going to dig it up and rehash it again. I fired Joe and he got another job. Now let it drop, understand? Joe stole some money, but I'm not hurt and I'm not crying. Let it go at that."

But he wouldn't look straight at Ed as he spoke. He looked at his toes instead.

Ed pondered his words and his manner. Breen had done Joe an injustice. His guilt over it took a strange form, that of hatred for Joe, and this hatred seemed to be increased by his shame in knowing his own son was the guilty one.

Then, at sixteen, Joe began seeing Molly Ledbetter again.

Almost a grown-up lady she was now. And Joe almost a grown-up man.

A dance at the Hall, twelve miles up the canyon. And a buggy ride home in the moonlight, with Joe a little high with liquor, and Molly, steadfast Molly, still loving him as she always had done.

The Hall was a log building with a single room in front, a small kitchen in the rear. Built as a community project by the ranchers in the canyon, it was a favorite location for the community dances. This one was to raise funds for the Community Women's Club.

Joe didn't take Molly to the dance. She went with Willie Breen. Joe went with four or five of D Diamond's other punchers.

Benches lined the wall, and upon them sat the older women and men, their children grouped around them. Sometimes a baby would cry. Sometimes a youngster would run and slide across the freshly waxed floor.

Polite restraint at first. But outside, every rig held a bottle, and you could always find a group around at least one of these rigs, passing the bottle around.

Joe stayed with his own crowd, drinking with them, joking with them. Occasionally he danced with one or another of the girls who were there, but never with Molly. He watched her, though, thinking she was the prettiest thing he had ever seen.

Tonight she had on a new, pale-green organdie dress that swirled stiffly around her trim ankles, that held her tight at the bodice, revealing modestly her full young breasts.

Molly never passed the group Joe was in without casting a shy, hasty glance at his face. Willie Breen danced most of the dances with her, holding her too tight, so that Joe and the rest of the country would think she was his.

And the town had got to Joe, had finally impressed upon him the feeling that he wasn't much account, even if he hadn't gone bad the way they said he would. He was too diffident to ask Molly to dance.

So Molly asked him.

She waited until the evening was well along, hoping he would come across the floor to her. He didn't, so at eleven, when it became apparent he was not going to, she excused herself a moment from Willie, pleading that she might be needed in the kitchen to help prepare the refreshments.

She was not needed, so she returned to the dance floor, avoiding Willie with deft skill, and heading straight for the corner where Joe Redenko stood with a group of other young punchers.

Her face was pale with fright, but her fine back was straight and defiant, and her steps were firm and proud. If her lower lip trembled slightly, it was not noticeable. She stopped immediately in front of Joe, who was talking to the young man beside him.

"Joe."

He turned, and his face darkened with confusion. "Hi, Molly."

"Aren't you going to ask me to dance?"

"Well, I . . ."

"Then I'll ask you. Dance with me, Joe."

A chuckle, muffled but audible, sounded behind Joe. He swung around, his eyes blazing. The chuckle died. He turned back to Molly. "Sure. I was goin' to ask you next dance."

He took her hand and put his right arm about her slim waist.

She looked up as they danced away. "You weren't really going to ask me, Joe."

"No. I guess not."

"Why? Don't you like me as well as those other girls you danced with?"

Joe wasn't used to the confusion he was feeling. His face felt hot and sweaty. He held Molly gingerly, as though she would break. "Sure I like you."

It was Molly's turn for embarrassment, but she didn't hesitate. "Then hold me as if you did. I won't break, Joe."

He'd had about four drinks. Not enough to affect his equilibrium, but enough to make him reckless. His arm tightened around her waist, and he drew her body against him.

It was soft, warm, and pliant. Her hair, fragrant and soft, brushed his cheek and tickled his nose.

An image of her father, Roscoe Ledbetter, formed in his mind, along with the remembered words "Stay away from her or I'll knock your damned hunky head off."

Defiantly Joe's arm tightened about her.

Then the dance was over. Flushed, excited, Joe stepped away from Molly, still holding her hand. Her eyes were upon his face, soft and vulnerable. She waited, and Joe knew she waited, for him to ask for the next dance. He thought of Willie Breen, and the old defiance came back. He said, "How about the next?"

The waiting in Molly stopped, and she seemed to relax almost imperceptibly. But her eyes stayed on his face. She asked, "How have you been, Joe? I've missed seeing you around town."

"Busy out at D Diamond."

"They say you're good at working cattle."

"Who says? Nobody in town would say that."

The faintest of smiles touched her face. "Well, they say that you're good, but . . ."

Joe had to return her smile. "I thought so. But. Someday I'll show 'em."

"I know you will."

The fiddler up on the stand at the front of the hall drew his bow across the strings. The piano player struck a chord.

Joe saw the alarm in Molly's eyes, heard her gasp of indrawn breath. His muscles tensed even before she got out the words "Joe! Look out!"

He started to whirl, from the corner of his eye seeing Molly instinctively step away. Then something hit him on the back of the neck, something numbing, paralyzing. He knew it was only a fist, even as he fell to the floor like a sledged steer.

He couldn't move, yet he could see and hear. His head

felt as if it would explode with pain.

Willie Breen, face twisted with hate, dived at him, landing with both knees in Joe's ribs. "Take my girl, will you? You hunky bastard, I'll kill you!"

The pain in Joe's chest was like a raging fire. He gasped for breath and discovered that he could move again. Feeling returned to his arms and legs, and he rolled his head aside to escape the raining blows Willie's fists drove at his face.

Strength returned, and Joe exploded into action, rolling, rising, flinging Willie from him. He came to his knees, and up to his feet in a crouch. Willie scrambled to his feet, his eyes panicking now.

Joe's fists drove out in short, wicked blows that turned Willie's face to a bleeding mass of torn flesh. The music stopped and the crowd formed a quick circle around the two. Someone yelled, "Hold on now, damn it, not in here! Take it outside!"

Willie went down, bleeding, near to unconsciousness. Joe went after him, pounding, hammering with merciless concentration.

His own D Diamond comrades pulled him away. "Joe! He's down. He's finished. Cut it out or you'll kill him."

A bitter laugh came from between Joe's teeth. There was more, much more to this than a sneak blow struck from behind. There were the words dredged out of Joe's memory, "Your ma's nothin' but a whore!" There was the memory of a false accusation of stealing. There was an endless, timeless antagonism that would live until one of these two was dead.

There were too many hands pulling Joe away, too many

hands upon his arms, restraining them. He stood away from Willie, and the hands released him.

He heard babbling voices of the crowd: ". . . disgraceful exhibition. Just what you'd expect from Mike Redenko's kid!" "He's dangerous. Someone ought to . . ." "We ought to have a sheriff's deputy at these dances to keep order. That's what we ought to have."

Joe felt a light touch on his arm, and looked down. Molly stood beside him, her face white with outrage. She said clearly, "Joe, will you take me home?"

"Sure." He shouldered a way roughly through the crowd, hating every one of them, and pulled her along behind.

But how? How would he take her home? In Willie's buggy? Riding double on his own horse, which bore a D Diamond brand on its hip?

They didn't speak until they were outside. Then she said, "That isn't Willie's buggy. It's Dad's."

Fine! Wonderful! Bring her home in Roscoe Ledbetter's buggy. He started to refuse, and then suddenly he grinned. "Your old man will have a stroke when he hears about it."

"Don't, Joe. Please."

"All right." He walked her across the bare yard to where the buggy was tied. He helped her into the seat, untied the horse, and climbed up beside her. He backed the horse out away from the tie rail. He got his own horse and tied him behind. Then he drove away.

For a while they rode in silence. Joe could feel his lip swelling where one of Willie's blows had landed, could feel the blood welling from half a dozen cuts on his face. He dragged out his bandanna and began to mop at the blood.

"Joe, pull up at the bridge. I'll wet a handkerchief in the

creek and get some of that blood off your face."

A mile farther on he pulled up. Molly jumped lightly down and stooped beside the creek to wet her handkerchief. Joe heard some horses coming down the road behind them, so he pulled the buggy off the road into the brush. Molly climbed in an instant before the horsemen passed.

For a moment they sat in conspiratorial silence. Then Molly laughed nervously. "Here, let me clean the blood off your face."

The handkerchief was cold and refreshing, the light touch of her hands soothing, but exciting too. Her fragrance wafted into his nostrils.

He made no conscious movement. But suddenly she was in his arms, arms that were strong with a young man's hunger, with a young man's need. Her mouth was soft, responsive against his own, and its sweetness fanned a fire that burned to his very depths.

Willing, loving Molly, to whom love could do no wrong. And Joe, as mixed up in his mind as a man could be, needing the spiritual quality of Molly's love as badly as he needed its physical manifestation.

He was awkward with her, but he was very tender in spite of the urgency that possessed him. He had not known that the world held anything as glorious as this that a man and woman could share, and, sharing, be bound together until one seemed inseparable from the other.

Afterward, he held her in his arms until the buggy seat became unendurable against his ribs. He sat up, releasing her and drawing away, aware at last of what he had done to her.

"Joe, what's the matter?"

"Nothin'. Nothin' at all." But his words were not convincing. He put his arms around her again, but this time there was no demand in the way they held her. He said hesitantly, "What I did wasn't right."

Molly was silent, stiffening suddenly in his arms. Joe could sense the hurt in her immediately. He said quickly, "What I did wasn't right, but I ain't sorry—at least, I'm not sorry if you're not."

"I'm not sorry, Joe. I love you, and love isn't just giving part of yourself. It's giving it all."

Joe swallowed. His throat burned, and so did his eyes. His arms tightened around her. He started to speak and stopped, and finally blurted, "I guess I love you too. I guess I've loved you for a long time, only I didn't know it."

She stirred in his arms, snuggling closer contentedly. He said, "We've got to get married now." At his words she stiffened again. Joe released her abruptly and sat up straight. He picked up the reins angrily, drew them tight, and clucked to the horse. He backed the buggy out into the road slowly so that his saddle horse, tied on behind, could stay out of its way.

Molly's voice was small. "Are you mad at me, Joe?"

"Mad? Why should I be mad?"

He looked at her defiantly. In the faint starlight, he could see her eyes glistening with unshed tears. Her voice was barely audible over the sound of the horse's hoofs. "I want to marry you, Joe, but I'm afraid. I'm afraid of what Pa might do to you."

Relief flooded through Joe. He'd been thinking . . . Well, he'd been thinking she didn't want to marry him because he was Joe Redenko. The old chip on his shoulder. He

70

should have known better. Who he was had never mattered to Molly before, and it didn't matter to her now.

He said, not very convincingly, "He won't do anything to me."

"Let's don't talk about it tonight. Please?" She moved close and laid her head against his shoulder.

They rode the rest of the trip in companionable silence. In town, he drove the buggy around in back of her house and unhitched. He turned the horse into the barn and fed him. When he came out, Molly was waiting in the dark and silent yard.

Joe kissed her. "When can I see you again? Saturday night?"

She nodded. "Any time you want, Joe."

"Will you meet me over behind the schoolhouse?"

"All right, Joe." She reached up, kissed him quickly on the mouth, and ran into the house.

Joe mounted his horse and headed out of town toward Dalhart's ranch. He thought about Molly, smiling. He loved her, all right. He sure enough did. And he'd be seeing her again. For now, that was enough.

CHAPTER EIGHT

Beginning that night, a new force went to work on Joe. It was a force with which he'd had little experience, the force of love.

He found it difficult to keep his mind on his work. And he found it doubly difficult to chart a course for himself into the future.

Molly loved him. She'd told him so, in words and in

actions. But she had also refused to marry him.

Her father's hatred of Joe had not lessened, he knew. And sooner or later, Roscoe Ledbetter would find out what was going on. When he did . . . Joe shuddered involuntarily. He admitted that he was still afraid of Ledbetter, sickeningly so. Perhaps the fears of a boy are never quite overcome in manhood.

He couldn't fight Ledbetter, either. His gun, with which he was surprisingly proficient, was not the answer. To kill Ledbetter would be to lose Molly forever. To kill Ledbetter with his fists was out of the question.

Unable to find the answer, Joe drifted. He saw Molly every Saturday night, but their meetings were necessarily secret. Molly was under no illusions as to what her father would do if he discovered that she was seeing Joe. He'd raved and stormed and ranted over the simple circumstance of Joe's bringing Molly home from the dance, without knowing or suspecting the further complications that had occurred when they stopped beside the stream to bathe Joe's face.

Sometimes when Molly thought of that night, her face would flush momentarily as though with shame. And yet she was not really ashamed, nor was she sorry. She'd loved Joe as long as she could remember, and to Molly love was not a thing to be given stingily or with reservations.

Reassuring to her was the almost desperate way Joe begged her to marry him.

"Joe, I can't!" she would say tearfully. "Don't you see? Pa would . . . well, he'd do something terrible to you. I know it. I know what an awful temper he has and how he hates you."

"I ain't afraid of him." But Joe's voice was only defiant, not convinced.

"I am, Joe. So please, let's just be happy together while we can."

He conceded the point angrily. "I just don't like hiding and sneaking around. I'm proud of you and of the way we feel. And I'm scared, Molly. If I don't marry you now . . ." He didn't finish. But both he and Molly knew what the finish would have been.

So they drifted. It was their custom to meet now at a spot downriver where there was a wide, looping bend in the stream and to which humans seldom went unless they were searching for lost stock. In the bend was one of the river's many islands that could be reached afoot if you didn't mind getting your feet wet. Molly always took off her shoes and stockings, hoisted her skirt to her knees, and waded across. Joe splashed across on horseback, and when it was time to go home, he carried her back across his saddle.

There was magic for Joe in these evenings with Molly— the magic of being loved, wanted, needed. The proud joy of being respected and admired. The heady intoxicant of being made to feel important.

Jake Dalhart noticed that Joe was always missing on Saturday nights between seven and eight-thirty. Knowing that Joe left the ranch at six, he made the obvious deduction immediately.

Another man would have grinned knowingly and let it pass. Not Dalhart. Dalhart's mind was too lecherous, too curious. So one night he followed Joe to watch.

From the concealment of the heavy willows along the river's bank, he saw Joe splash across to the island. Later, he saw Molly Ledbetter wade across, shoes in hand, skirt hoisted to her pretty knees.

Dalhart grinned delightedly. Well, I'll be damned. Her! The banker's girl! Wait till I see Joe. Will I give him a ridin', the sly bastard!

It did not even occur to him that Joe might be in love with Molly. Love was an alien word in Dalhart's vocabulary, one to which he gave, when he used it, quite a different meaning than that generally given it. Perhaps he assumed that his own contempt for women was duplicated in Joe. Had not Joe's mother been a known prostitute? Did Joe have any good reason for loving and trusting the female sex?

Dalhart was in a congratulatory mood as Joe approached him later in the saloon. He grinned suggestively. "You're a sly bastard, Joe."

"What're you talking about?" Joe's face wore a puzzled, uneasy frown.

"Don't act dumb. I saw you sneak out to the island. I saw her sneak along after you."

"Nobody was sneakin'." Joe's voice was tight with anger.

"All right. All right. But tell me, Joe, how is she? Pretty good?" He fished a cigar from his pocket and lighted it, and so did not see the wild flare in Joe's eyes. He looked up, and then saw the flare, too late.

He tried to come to his feet. Joe's face was white. His eyes seemed to be on fire.

Dalhart sank back. He'd seen that look once or twice before, and he recognized it now. He made a sudden grab for his gun.

His hand made it to the polished walnut grips of the gun at his side, but he got no chance to draw it, let alone fire it, for Joe's fist smashed into his mouth, flattening his lips, loosening two of his front teeth. With blood gushing from his mouth and nose, Dalhart went backward in his chair, which skidded a few feet, teetered, then crashed to the floor.

Joe was upon him before he had stopped moving. The instep of Joe's boot came down with crushing force on Dalhart's right wrist and turned. Dalhart's gasp turned to a thin screech of pain. With the injured hand he clawed for his gun a second time, driven by fear that twisted his face into a grimace and made it almost unrecognizable.

Joe let him get the gun clear and then kicked it out of his hand. It skittered across the saloon floor and came up against the half-filled brass spittoon with a loud, tinny crash.

Joe stood over him, breathing shallowly through clenched teeth. His breath made a thin, whistling sound. His eyes were afire, his nostrils pinched and white, his jawline hard and taut as a steel cable. He said in a voice that was strange and terrible, "Get up, you dirty-mouthed bastard! Get up so I can take you apart!" All the disgust he had ever felt for Dalhart was in his face.

Dalhart's glance fled around the hushed saloon, plainly seeking support, and as plainly finding none. He said, "Joe . . ."

"Shut up! I've heard you stand over there and say all women were rotten. Well, they ain't! It's you that's rotten—all the way to your stinking core. You're a goddamn animal—a filthy, rotten animal."

Though he didn't know it, Joe had probed the sore that festered in Dalhart's brain. Hate flared in Dalhart's eyes, along with fury that turned his face livid. He averted his face and, trembling, deliberately fought down his fury. Then he lunged to his feet, driving himself toward Joe, driving the point of his shoulder upward between Joe's spraddled legs. "Git 'em there," he'd told Joe a hundred times, "where you can really hurt 'em, and you'll end the fight before it starts." For a moment, Joe had forgotten his teaching.

Almost too late, Joe remembered that Dalhart was the master of dirty fighting tactics and turned, catching Dalhart's blow only partly where it was aimed, partly on the front of one of his thighs. The force of the blow still got to him, but not with all its crippling power.

Joe grunted, twisting away to let Dalhart fall from the force of his own lunge. Joe's face twisted with the violence of his pain. He backstepped, waiting for the pain to ease, for his vision to clear. Pain had confused him, and he had the new and unexplainable feeling that he was fighting not only Jake Dalhart, but the whole town and every person in it. He was fighting for Molly, and he'd win, if he could have a little time for his head to clear.

Dalhart gave him no time. He came across the saloon floor in a furious rush, fists flailing, landing, missing, landing again.

Joe's face was white, and beads of sweat stood out upon it. He covered with his arms and elbows, taking the brunt of Dalhart's blows on them.

Gone from Dalhart's face was the earlier fear that had shown there. Now it contained a certain sureness as though he again saw Joe as a kid used to taking orders, young and inexperienced, who could be beaten in spite of the fury that still burned in his eyes—honestly beaten, perhaps, but more easily beaten by a ruse.

Gasping from his savage exertion, Dalhart dropped his hands and whined, "Cut it out, Joe. Hell, I didn't mean nothin' by what I said."

Uncertainty passed across Joe's eyes like a cloud across the sky. Dalhart said, "Come on. I'll buy a drink an' we'll forget all about it, huh?"

And then, while Joe stood panting, turning this over in his mind, Dalhart plunged his right, with all the force of his wiry body behind it, into Joe's stomach.

Joe doubled, caught completely off guard. As his head came down, Dalhart clasped his hands together and brought the two of them against the back of Joe's neck like a weighted club.

Joe went down soddenly, striking the floor with his face. He was down; he was beat, and not because Dalhart was the better man, but only because Joe had been a fool. A fool to trust anyone, anyone at all in the world save himself.

He thought his spine would crack with the force of Dalhart's boot toe crashing against it. A sharp groan of pain escaped his lips. But his eyes were blind and his head was filled with fog. His limbs were lead, his muscles watery and weak.

Again Dalhart's boot toe smashed into his inert body.

Joe's rage began to stir again, until each of Dalhart's kicks was like more dry wood heaped upon the fires of fury.

He rolled, covering, and crawled away from Dalhart's kicks like a whipped and beaten dog. Indeed, he resembled one until you saw his eyes. There was no defeat in his eyes, no acceptance.

But Dalhart didn't see his eyes. In a frenzy of savage satisfaction, he kept kicking Joe, trying to break his ribs, trying to crush his face.

It went on until the onlookers grew sick from the brutality of it. But with each passing moment, more and more of Joe's strength returned. His brain power, which had been stunned and stilled by Dalhart's two-fisted blow against the back of his neck, came sharply back.

At last the moment Joe had been awaiting came. Dalhart, exhausted by his own efforts, by his own emotion, paused to rest, breathing heavily.

Joe's recovery amazed the onlookers, for he had looked half dead. But Joe was not beaten. No man is ever beaten until his spirit breaks.

Joe came to his knees, head hanging. He rested a moment then came unsteadily to his feet.

Once he thought he would fall. He staggered against a table and overturned it. But he caught another in time and stayed erect.

Dalhart looked on with pure amazement, still breathless.

Then Joe started toward him.

Slowly he came at first. But as he came his head went forward and his hands came up, forming fists. His knees steadied, and his face twisted into a grimace of hatred.

Line by line, you could have analyzed Dalhart's expression, and could not have said when it changed. But change it did, and Joe saw it. So did the others in Rafferty's saloon. They saw the savage satisfaction replaced by fear and a desire to run. They saw the eyes begin to shift like those of a cornered coyote.

Dalhart tried to fight, but he was no match for Joe's

almost maniacal fury. His face became a mass of blood and bruises. His body absorbed more punishment than a bucking horse can ever administer. He fell forward, and Joe's upthrusting knee was waiting to smash his face. He put his hands on the floor to force himself up, and Joe's boot came down on the knuckles, grinding, crushing.

Then Joe picked him up and threw him through the door. Rolling, Dalhart landed in the dust among the crowd that had collected to watch.

Pride fought with instinct in his battered face. Then the pride was gone, and only instinct remained, the strong, age-old instinct of self-preservation.

Blood and spittle drooled from his mouth as he turned his travesty of a face upward toward Joe. "Please, for God's sake, please! Don't hit me again! Don't kill me!"

Disgust touched Joe, as it touched every man who saw Dalhart. But not all of Joe's disgust was for Dalhart. Part of it was for himself, because when one man loses human dignity, so does every other man, particularly those who have been responsible, and those who have stayed to watch.

The crowd broke up, silent, failing to meet each other's eyes. Dalhart lay semi-conscious in the street, waiting until they should all be gone. And Joe headed for the river to bathe his bruised and bloody body in its cooling, soothing depths. Perhaps he also went to wash off some of the uncleanliness of his encounter with Dalhart.

Joe was certainly not a fool. Treading water in one of the river's deeper pools, he realized that he had earned another enemy, to go with Ledbetter and Breen.

They were three, now, and each of them hated him more than any man should hate another. How would Ledbetter's hatred express itself? How would Breen's? And how would Dalhart strike back at the man who had made him crawl and beg in the dry dust of the street for all the town to see?

Joe didn't know. But he was sure of two things: One was that he no longer had a job. The other was that Dalhart would find a way to strike back. Dalhart would surely find a way.

CHAPTER NINE

Joe soaked and swam in the river until the sun sank behind the great pile of clouds in the west. Then he got out on the bank, shook the water from his body like a dog, and put on his clothes.

Each small movement was torment. His body was red now in the places where Dalhart's kicks and blows had landed. But tomorrow those places would be blue-black.

His face was scabbed, but the water had softened the scabs and it began to bleed again. Joe dabbed at it with a red bandanna from his pocket.

He was strangely depressed, and perhaps this was the backwash of conflict, the depression that must inevitably follow such an expenditure of concentration and energy as the fight had consumed.

He got his horse, noticing the D Diamond brand on its hip. He rode through town, ignoring those in the streets, and dismounted at the stable behind Ed Mallory's house. Here he offsaddled and turned the horse loose. It wasn't his to use any more. His job at D Diamond was gone, a thing of the past.

He went in through the back door and crossed the

creaking porch. He stepped into the kitchen, and found Ed Mallory there.

Joe looked at Ed wearily. He said, "You hear about it?"

"The fight? Yeah, I heard." There was a certain weariness in Ed's voice too, as though he had faced Joe's trouble too often before.

Joe felt anger stir. "Well, what the hell would you have done?"

Ed snapped angrily, "Get the goddamn chip off your shoulder. I don't even know what it was about. Nobody else seems to either."

"It was about Jake's dirty mouth."

"And Molly?"

Joe glanced at him sharply. "Yeah. And Molly."

Ed met his eyes. "You've been seeing Molly, ain't you?"

"What if I have? Anything wrong with that?"

"Is there, Joe? You tell me."

Joe's eyes met Ed's hard ones steadily. He said tightly, "I'm tellin' you. There's nothin' wrong. I'm in love with her and her with me. I want to marry her, but she won't agree. She's afraid of what her old man would do to me. She figures her old man would go haywire if he even knew we were seeing each other."

"He'll know now. Dalhart will tell him."

"If Dalhart opens his dirty mouth I'll give him some more of what I gave him tonight."

Ed shrugged. "All right, Joe. Now how about some supper?"

Joe ate in scowling silence. Why did nothing ever seem to go right? Why couldn't he be like other young men, court the girl he wanted, marry her, and work his life away to support her and make her happy? Why did it always have to be this way, everything wrong, everything devious, secret, and somehow shameful?

His face turned bitter as his mind told him the answer: Because you're Joe Redenko. Because your pa was a drunk, and murdered your mother because she was a . . . His mind couldn't say the word.

Ed finished his coffee and lighted a cigarette. Outside, the sky was dark, clouded over and without stars. Joe said, "Think I'll go for a walk."

Ed didn't speak. Joe went out the door and into the night.

In the stable, a horse stirred and nickered softly. Somewhere in the yard a cricket chirped. The town noises came to Joe's ears, a dog barking at the coyotes yipping up near the rim, a baby crying, a man shouting harshly at his wife, who occasionally shrilled back.

Somewhere in town a piano haltingly played hymns, and a clear young voice sang. The hymns made Joe think of Ledbetter, and he frowned.

He didn't know where he was going, but he found his steps taking him toward the Ledbetter house, a big two-storied white frame house out at the edge of the town beside the cemetery.

Why he went there, he wasn't sure. Perhaps it was because he could feel closer to Molly. Perhaps he hoped to see her through the lighted bay window of the living room.

He stood across the street from the Ledbetter house in the shelter of a cottonwood. His body was stiffening now, and each small movement hurt him, so he tried to be still.

After a while he saw the front door open, and Ledbetter came out. The man went down the walk, opened the picket gate, and stepped out into the street. He was smoking a cigar, which he now threw away.

In spite of himself, Joe trembled inwardly as Ledbetter's eyes touched the place where he stood. But Ledbetter apparently saw nothing, for he turned and headed down the street. Joe waited until he was out of sight, then went through the gate and across the lawn toward the house.

Molly was sitting in the living room, some knitting in her lap. Joe tapped lightly on the window and she looked up and saw him.

At once her glance went with fright around the room. Then it calmed and she got up and came out. Behind her, in the house, a woman's voice called, "Is that you, Molly? Where are you going?"

"Just out in the yard. It's cooler there."

She came across the lawn to where Joe stood in the shadow of a weeping willow tree. "Joe! What happened to you?"

"Fight with Dalhart. He knows about us."

"But why did you fight?"

"It doesn't matter."

"Was it something about me?"

"Just something he said. The important thing is that now I haven't got a job any more."

She touched his cheek in sympathy. "What will you do?"

"Find another, I guess."

"You're bitter, aren't you?"

"Maybe I am. Do you blame me? Now Ed's got to ask somebody else to give me a job. But what's going to happen when Ed runs out of people to ask? I wish you'd marry me and go away with me. I got a little money.

We'd make out."

"I know that, Joe. And I want to! But he'd follow us. He'd find us no matter where we went. He hates you so terribly, Joe, that it scares me. I think he'd kill you if he knew about us. Why does Pa hate you so? You've never done anything to hurt him."

Joe said, "I don't know why he hates me." But he knew.

Molly stood close to him looking up. Her eyes were shy, but not hesitant. She was offering him something, offering herself. Some age-old woman's wisdom told her that tonight he needed her, that she could ease the torment within him. Her glance lay upon his face like a soft caressing hand.

It was perhaps a moment when Joe himself should have been strong, insistent, when he should have picked her up and carried her away. He should have carried her to the town's preacher and married her in spite of her protests.

But he was filled with the pain of his hurts, the torment of his confusion. He was plagued with doubts. Molly's persistent refusals to marry him had made him unsure of her, unsure of himself, and troubled about the future. He was willing to face Ledbetter's wrath. Why, then, wasn't Molly also willing? Was there another reason for her refusal, a reason she had not told him?

He stood, tense and cold, looking down at her.

Her face lost something of its animation and became oddly still. She said at last, "I have to go in, Joe. Mother will be coming out if I don't. Good luck at finding a new job. Will I see you Saturday?"

"Sure. Sure you will. Same place?" But his voice was preoccupied and not fully concerned with her now.

"Yes, Joe. Same place." She turned and went into the house, looking oddly dejected.

He watched for a long time after she disappeared, his mind seeing her, soft, vital beauty. Then he scowled. Why couldn't the damned town let him alone?

He turned and went through the gate. He wandered down the street, directionless, thinking. He paused to shape a cigarette. When he had it finished, he stuck it into his mouth and fished in his pocket for a match.

He heard a door close, a woman's soft voice: "Good night, darling."

Steps came down the walk of the house before which Joe stood. He saw the bulk of a man. . . .

Suddenly Joe felt as though he were no longer a man, but again a little boy waiting outside the house to talk to one of his mother's callers—Ledbetter. There was something all too familiar in that bulky figure, in the cautious yet confident walk.

And there was something familiar about the woman's voice, which seemed to echo back and forth in Joe's mind.

He tried to step back, tried to remain unseen, but he wasn't quick enough. He was standing but a yard from the gate when Ledbetter opened it.

Ledbetter saw him, made a quick move toward him. Joe said quickly, "Oh, no! Not again. I'm not a little kid any more."

Ledbetter made a choking sound. At a walk that was almost a run, he brushed past Joe and went down the street.

Up on the porch, the door opened again and a woman went in. The door closed behind her, but not before Joe recognized her in the square of light formed by the open door.

85

It was Susan Poole, Ledbetter's clerk at the bank.

Joe's lip twisted. So this was the one who had replaced his mother after she died? So this was the one? His mother's death had not changed Ledbetter, had not killed the lusts, the needs that burned in his twisted soul.

Joe grinned shakily, thinking that if Ledbetter had hated him before, he now hated him twice as savagely. Because again Joe had discovered his secret. And again Joe must serve as Ledbetter's unwilling conscience.

In spite of himself, Joe could not help feeling a little sorry for the man, because Joe himself had known frustration in the past weeks. He had known the guilt of enforced secrecy. He had known helplessness.

He turned and walked toward home, discouraged and depressed. He was being blamed again for what his mother had been. Ledbetter was, he knew, assigning to Joe the moral weakness that had been Sonja's. Feeling this way, Ledbetter would never consent to Joe's and Molly's marriage. Never in a million years.

CHAPTER TEN

Angry voices awoke Joe next morning. For a moment he lay in his bed, groggy with sleep, and listened to their loud but so far indistinguishable sounds coming to him through the house. Both were recognizable, for he knew both well. One belonged to Roscoe Ledbetter, the other to Ed Mallory.

Joe's mind grasped the import of the argument almost at once. The worst apparently had happened. Dalhart had got to Ledbetter.

Joe swung his feet to the floor. Hastily he dragged on his

pants, and, slipping into a shirt, still barefooted, he opened his door and headed for the kitchen.

He could hear the voices more plainly now. Ledbetter was saying angrily, "Get out of my way, Ed. Get out of my way before I kill you too."

Ed's voice was lower, calmer. "Don't be a goddamn fool. You're not going past me into the house. You're going to get yourself shot if you keep on trying."

Joe stopped in the hallway, struggling with himself. He wanted to show himself, to face Ledbetter, but he knew that if he did, Ledbetter's fury would grow beyond Ed's ability to handle it. No doubt Ledbetter had a gun, and would use it if Joe appeared.

Something within Joe whispered, Well, why not? Either he'll get me or Ed will get him.

But he didn't move, knowing he would be being unfair to Ed if he did.

There was a moment's silence out there. Then Joe heard the impact of a body against the wall of the house.

He jumped into the kitchen, ready now for whatever he might see. He saw Ed, pinned against the doorjamb by the bulk of Ledbetter's body. He saw the shotgun in Ledbetter's hands.

Ledbetter saw him at the same instant. Wrath flared in the man's eyes, and he strove desperately to bring the shotgun muzzle to bear.

A shotgun! Joe had seen what a shotgun could do at close range. And there was no avoiding the blast. Even poorly aimed, it was bound to get him.

He dived for the floor, at the same instant that Ed recovered and came thrusting himself away from the doorjamb.

Ed's hands went out, flung upward against the gun muzzle.

The gun roared, filling the room with an intolerable volume of sound, with acrid, biting smoke, and the charge, tearing into the ceiling, caused a rain of plaster and dust.

Rolling, miraculously untouched, Joe squinted at the doorway in time to see Ed's revolver clear its holster. Up it came, and the barrel came down against the top of Ledbetter's head with an audible crack.

Ledbetter staggered out into the middle of the room, still conscious. The shotgun slipped from his grasp and struck the floor, and the second charge roared out.

Like a skyrocket the gun skittered across the floor and came to rest against the wall with a thump. The charge tore into the floor, missing Joe by a scant margin of inches. But the shotgun was harmless now. Trembling, Joe got to his feet.

Ledbetter was on his knees, shaking his head. Ed Mallory stood over him, gun in hand. "Roscoe, by God, you're going to jail. You're going to face a charge of attempted murder. What in the hell gave you the notion you could kill someone for seeing your daughter?"

Ledbetter's face was pale. His hand went up to rub the knot Ed had put on his hard head. For an instant he seemed confused, and he looked at Joe as though he were wondering why he hated this boy so much. For the first time he seemed to be seeing Joe as he was, instead of the way his own mind had made him. He looked away, something like shame in his eyes.

Joe said, "No, Ed. Let him go. I don't want Molly's name dragged through court. It'd ruin her."

Ledbetter probably could have tolerated anything from

Joe but this. Anger, hatred, resentment he could have stood. But not this. Not magnanimity from Joe Redenko. The shame was gone suddenly from his eyes, replaced by the old hatred. He seemed to be trying to find words dirty enough to use on Joe. Surprisingly, his voice came out without profanity, but utterly contemptuous. "You think she isn't ruined now? You filthy, dirty Polack!" He paused, still unable to find a word bad enough to describe Joe. "I'll kill you before I'll let you see her again! You stay in town and try, and by the Almighty God, I'll kill you!"

Sweat stood out in beads on his face, which was a ghastly shade of gray. Suddenly, surprisingly, he retched, bending double and gagging, sickened by the very intensity of his hatred.

Ed Mallory's face was a study of revulsion, as though he had found a poisonous snake on his kitchen floor. He toed Ledbetter with his boot, and his voice was thin and cold. "Get up and get out of here, before I do some killin' myself! Go on, get out!"

Ledbetter got up and stumbled out, with a last vitriolic glance at Joe.

Ed watched him go from the door, then shuddered slightly and turned back to Joe. "My God, boy, what did you ever do to him to earn that? There's a hell of a lot more to it than your seeing Molly. Is the girl pregnant?"

Joe shook his head, angry, sickened himself. He could have told Ed then why Ledbetter hated him. But he knew it would serve no purpose. He had reached the end of his road here in Du Bois. It was get out now or face Ledbetter's killing fury again.

He tried to find some reason, some sense in the confusion

of his thoughts. Was he afraid? He admitted that he was. Ledbetter was insane with hatred.

But it wasn't fear of dying so much that bothered Joe. It was fear that if he stayed he'd end up killing Ledbetter. And he knew that would be the end of everything.

Joe said, "Will you let me have a horse?"

"Anything I've got is yours, Joe. You know that."

"Then get the roan saddled while I pack some things."

Ed hesitated for the shortest instant. Then obediently he went out of the house and headed for the stable.

Joe glanced at the floor where Ledbetter had been and his nose wrinkled with distaste. Then he went back to the bedroom and pulled on his boots. Afterward he went out to the pump and washed vigorously, as though trying to scrub something unclean from his soul.

He went back into the house, stuffed some food into a sack. He made a blanket roll with a couple of blankets, putting the sack of food in the center of it. He strapped on his gun and belt, and, carrying the bedroll, went out to the stable.

Ed had the roan saddled, and another horse for himself. "I'll ride a ways with you, Joe."

Joe shrugged and mounted the roan. "Ed, I've been trying to get Molly to marry me. She won't because she's afraid of what her old man would do to me if she did. But see her, will you? Tell her I'll write when I get settled and have a stake big enough for us to get started on. Tell her she can't go through life being scared of what someone else might do. You can convince her."

"I'll convince her, Joe."

They rode for awhile in silence, heading downriver

toward the canyon. Joe's eyes touched the cottonwoods that marked the river's bend and the island where he'd known so many happy hours with Molly. They touched the island where he'd hidden after his mother's death. Later they touched another island, the one where Big Mike had been killed.

All of Joe's life, the good and the bad, seemed tied together by the river and its tiny, brush-choked islands. He felt depressed, defeated.

At the mouth of the canyon he stopped, looked at Ed. "You'd better go back."

Ed nodded. "I suppose so. What will you do?"

Joe shrugged. "What any man does, I suppose. Find a job." His voice grew bitter, angry. "Or maybe, by God, I won't find a job. Maybe I'll do it another way. I've tried it their way. I've tried hard work and honesty, and what the hell has it got me?"

Ed said, "You're sour now. You're mad at everybody. Don't stay that way, Joe. It'll get you nothin' but trouble in the end."

Joe laughed harshly. "More than I've got already?"

Ed nodded. "More than you've got already." His eyes, looking at Joe, were gloomy, defeated. Finally he shrugged. "You've got plenty to be bitter about. But bitterness is a damned poor way of life."

"Maybe. Maybe not."

Ed's expression was glum. Joe knew he was groping for words that would help Joe bear the emptiness of leaving, the loneliness that would torture him in the months to come. But Ed found no words.

Joe touched his heels to the roan's ribs and moved away.

He waved at Ed, but he didn't smile. "So long, Ed."

Going around the bend in the narrow road, Joe turned and looked back. He was too far away to read the expression on Ed's face, but the slump of Ed's body was eloquent of hopelessness, of foreboding.

Joe felt a rising resentment. Now even Ed was against him. He turned and rode into the canyon. To hell with them. To hell with them all. From here on Joe would ride his own trail, with no interference from anybody. From here on, Joe himself would determine which direction it took.

CHAPTER ELEVEN

Joe, man-grown though he might be, was still only sixteen, going on seventeen. This was the first time he had ridden away from all the familiar things that to him meant home. And even though he had found little good in his early years, there was still a kind of umbilical cord that had tied him to them. But the cord was cut now and the wind of the outer world was cold upon him.

Night came, and Joe offsaddled and took care of his horse. He ate sparingly of the food he had brought, longing for coffee to go with it. With his saddle for a pillow, with his gun nearby, he rolled himself in his blankets and tried to sleep.

But sleep would not come. He thought of Molly, and longed for her softness and compassion beside him. And he made a vow eternal in angry youth: I'll show 'em. I'll come back rich and then see what they say.

But how to get rich? Riding for some cattle outfit at thirty a month? Clerking in a store for twenty?

Joe fell asleep at last, and woke up half frozen as dawn began to gray along the eastern horizon.

He passed through a couple of small settlements and one fair-sized town that day without stopping except once to buy some supplies.

And the next night he camped, again beside the river, near to the broad reach of desert that lay on both sides of the Colorado-Utah border.

He built a fire and heated water in the new coffeepot he'd bought that day. He threw in a handful of coffee. When it had boiled awhile he set it aside and added a little cold water to settle the grounds.

Then he cooked his meat, a piece of beef he'd bought. Its smell was savory, rising on the still air. He settled down on his heels to watch it cook.

Suddenly he heard a twig snap. The sound meant but one thing to him: game, meat for tomorrow and the days to come. He reached for the gun at his side.

A voice said sharply, "Uh-uh. Don't do it, son."

Joe started, but he brought his hand away from the gun. He looked toward the sound of the voice.

A man stood there, the lower half of him hidden by brush. He held a revolver negligently in his hand, but its muzzle was trained unerringly on Joe's chest.

Joe said, a shade angrily because he had started so violently, "What the hell do you want?"

"Just to stay alive, boy. That's all. How come you're so jumpy?"

"I thought it might be a deer."

The man chuckled. He called over his shoulder, "All right, Claude. You can come out."

93

He holstered the revolver and stepped out of the brush toward Joe. A moment later, another man came from behind him. The two of them stood looking down at Joe, grinning.

The first one, the big one, was a hulking bear of a man, with close-set eyes of a cold gray color. His face was tanned dark, oily with sweat, and covered with a week's growth of black whiskers. His lips were full, but somehow too perpetually smiling to be attractive.

The second was smaller, thinner, and wore a mustache that was almost ridiculously long. This one's face held a mocking, sardonic expression.

The big one said, "Coffee hot?"

Joe nodded. He felt uncomfortable in the presence of their grinning amusement, as though they mocked him in their thoughts for his age, his inexperience.

The big one walked away, saying over his shoulder, "I'll bring the horses up."

"All right, Noah." The little one, Claude, watched Joe intently with the same sardonic expression. The meat was burning in the skillet, so he drew a long knife from his belt, speared it, and turned it over. He wiped the blade carefully on his greasy pants before returning it to its sheath.

After a few moments, Noah returned with two horses. Both were sweated and caked with dust. Their heads hung wearily and dejectedly, and they did not even try to crop grass. Joe guessed they'd been ridden today to the point of exhaustion.

He took another quick look at the men, and felt a stir of excitement. Outlaws. That's what they were. Outlaws on the dodge. Everything about them shouted it, from the guns hanging low at their sides to their frayed clothing, their beat horses.

Noah said, "Nice of you to invite us to supper. We're hungry as hell, I don't mind tellin' you. Anything else in that sack there?"

"Beans. Some bread."

"Break it out. We ain't et all day."

Joe felt a stir of resentment, but he didn't argue. He fished two cans of beans from the sack, and the crushed loaf of bread. He wondered if they'd rob him when they were through eating.

Claude opened the cans expertly with his knife and dumped the beans into the skillet with the meat. Noah got two tin cups from his saddle and filled them with coffee. As an afterthought he poured Joe's cup full. Then he got a flat brown whisky bottle from his saddlebags and dumped a generous portion into each cup.

He handed Joe his cup and said, "Appreciate the supper. Here, try this—for your appetite."

Joe sipped the spiked coffee. Hell, what did they think, that he hadn't ever had a drink before?

The meat and beans were done. Claude cut the meat into three equal chunks with his knife, and ladled out the beans by shoving them out of the skillet with its blade. He began to eat wolfishly, using only his fingers and the knife. Noah did likewise.

Joe didn't have a knife, so he used the spoon he'd bought today. He finished and settled back comfortably. He was more at ease with the strangers now. All they'd wanted was something to eat. And Joe was glad to have company.

He asked, "Where you from? And where you headin'?"

Noah smiled his perpetual smile. He tossed his head toward the south. "Come from there. Goin' there." He tossed his head toward the north.

"Ridin' out tonight?"

"Uh-uh. The hosses are beat. We'll bunk here tonight— that is, if you ain't got no objection."

"Help yourself."

The fire died, and the light faded from the western sky. Joe got out his blankets and rolled himself in them beside the remains of the fire. Noah and Claude made their beds farther away, perhaps twenty yards back in the brush.

Joe knew it was their habitual caution that made them bunk so far away. An outlaw's habitual caution. It wouldn't do to be caught right beside the fire. Anybody knew that.

Inside, Joe was secretly thrilled to be consorting, even for so short a time, with a pair of desperados. And for the first time since leaving Du Bois, his mind forgot Ledbetter, his flight from town, his loneliness and solitary misery. He went to sleep almost at once.

He never knew quite what it was that awakened him. But awake, he lay still, listening.

Suddenly he heard a whispered voice, the soft nicker of a horse, the crack of a twig under a horse's hoof.

Why were they leaving so soon?

Suddenly Joe's mind put it all together. He knew why they were leaving so early. They were stealing his horse.

He remembered the heavy loads that had been packed behind each of their saddles. He remembered the pack-saddle tree and panniers that had bunched so high behind Claude's saddle. They wanted Joe's horse for a pack horse, obviously having lost their own.

Oddly enough, fear didn't touch Joe at all. Only anger. Hell, he'd fed them at the expense of his own breakfast. He'd trusted them. And this was how they repaid him.

He rolled cautiously, untangling himself from his blankets. He got to his feet without pulling on his boots. He loosened his gun in its holster, then as an afterthought drew it and carefully thumbed back the hammer. Then, walking cautiously, he headed toward the spot from which had come the noise. Underfoot, the ground was littered with small rock and pieces of brush that hurt Joe's bare feet. But he managed to walk without making any noise.

He saw their blending, darker shapes against the lighter color of the brush behind them. Three large shadows, and that would be the horses. One elongated, tall shadow that would be Noah. Joe couldn't see Claude, and guessed he was either in front of one of the horses or behind, so that his form was hidden.

It was a chance Joe didn't like to take, not knowing where Claude was. And suddenly he was frightened. But his anger was greater than his fear. He said, "Hold it. Right where you are."

There was a violent flurry of movement beside the horses. One of them lunged away, ran a few yards, and stopped. Noah's gun flamed, and Joe flung a shot at the flare. Even before he heard Noah's sharply indrawn breath, he was changing position so that a shot at the flare of his own gun wouldn't get him.

The shot came, from Claude's gun, and it cut through the brush where Joe had been standing a moment before.

Suddenly Joe's fear was gone. They couldn't see him. Perhaps their eyes were not so sharp as his, perhaps just not so young. Joe chuckled. He liked the sound and chuckled again. "Take your own horses and get the hell out of here. Leave mine alone."

Noah's voice boomed back at him, and it held a certain whining quality. "Kid, you've got it wrong. We wasn't stealin' your horse. We was just gettin' our own."

There was pain noticeable in Noah's voice, in its tightness, in the sharp, clipped way his words came out. Joe didn't say anything, so Noah went on: "You hit me, kid. I can't travel now. Hell, we want to be friends with you. We wouldn't steal nothin' from you. Ain't that right, Claude?"

"Hell, yes. What Noah says is so, kid."

Noah whined again, "Go build up the fire, that's a good kid. I'm bleedin' to death."

But Joe was suspicious now. He shook his head, though they could not see him in the darkness. "Throw your guns over this way. Them knives, too. Then I reckon Claude can build up the fire while I watch."

There was a moment's hesitation. Finally Noah muttered, "Well, I reckon that's fair enough, Claude. Ain't it?"

"Sure. Sure." Claude seemed to have been waiting for a cue of some kind. Joe's hand tightened on his gun. "Throw your guns over this way."

He heard them fall. One. Two. "Now the knives."

These thuds were fainter, but he counted two. "Now get on over to the fire. I'll be watching."

"Do like he says, Claude. I ain't in shape for no foolishness."

Joe saw them go past, ten yards away. He followed cautiously. Claude busied himself with the fire while Noah sank down on the ground. In the first flare of the match, Joe noticed that Noah held a lumpy hand against his side inside the shirt.

Claude bent over him. "Let me look."

"Nothin' but a furrow. Didn't cut through. But Jesus, I'm bleedin' like a stuck hog."

Joe slipped away and looked at the horses. His own roan carried the pack saddle. They'd meant to steal the roan, just as he had thought.

He returned to the fire, his awe of the two gone, in its place a kind of contempt. He had learned something these last few moments. It was that a man outside the law can never trust a living soul except himself.

He said, "You're a pair of liars. The pack saddle's on my roan."

Noah grinned his perpetual grin, but it was weak and without humor. Claude looked at Joe out of careful, unwinking eyes, his sardonic expression gone. Noah asked finally, "So?"

"So I'm moving on. Right now."

"Most kids your age wouldn't have had the guts to try an' stop us. They'd have let the horse go."

"Maybe. What does that prove?"

Noah said heartily, "Nothin', maybe. Maybe a lot. I like you, kid. Stick with us a while an' maybe we can do you some good."

Joe laughed.

Noah said, "Don't believe it, do you? But listen. You've run away from home, ain't you? You ain't got much money, I'll bet, an' no job. All right. We got plenty of money. Part of it's yours. Just stick with us till I can travel again. Ride into town once in a while after supplies. Call it a job if you want, but we'll sure as hell make it worth your while."

Joe didn't speak. Noah grunted, "Claude, get the saddle-bags. Give the kid a couple hundred." He looked at Joe. "Will that put you easy in your mind about your horse? Hell, suppose we do steal him? You can buy three horses with the two hundred, can't you?"

Joe nodded, still suspicious. He kept his gun trained on Claude as the little man went to the horses and removed the saddlebags, which seemed to be heavy. Claude reached inside and brought out a handful of gold. He counted out ten double eagles and held them out to Joe.

Noah asked, "Well, what do you say?"

Joe took the money and holstered his gun. "What have I got to lose?" Indeed, what did he have to lose? Here was more money than he could make in six months punching cows. He hadn't compromised his honesty to get it, either. A few more windfalls like this and he could send for Molly.

He let himself dwell on that, feeling important, smart, knowing Molly would think he was smart too. And he was proud of himself. He hadn't let them get away with his horse and they respected him for it. Maybe they were out-laws. Maybe they had stolen the money. But Joe hadn't had anything to do with stealing it. And maybe if he did a good job of looking after them while Noah healed, they'd give him more.

He asked, "What's the closest town? I'll head in now after some more grub."

Claude looked at him suspiciously, but Noah grinned. "That's the stuff. I reckon Hobson, Utah, is the closest. About ten-twelve miles down the river. We're going to move back in the hills a piece. Can you follow sign?"

Joe nodded.

Noah said, "Don't try trailin' us from here, because there won't be no sign. You'll pick up our trail over there." He gestured toward the low, bare hills that footed the mesa to the north. "Just ride north along the foot of them hills until you find our tracks."

Joe nodded again. Noah said, "An' kid, get some whisky, too, will you? Give him some more money, Claude."

Joe said, "My name's Joe, not kid."

"Sure, Joe. Sure."

Claude gave Joe two more gold pieces. Joe took the pack saddle off the roan, saddled, mounted, and rode out. Behind him Claude and Noah began to argue in careful, subdued tones.

CHAPTER TWELVE

Ed Mallory looked across at Joe in the deep gray light that now filtered in from outside the cabin. "So that's how you got tied up with the Allen boys?"

Joe nodded. "I was mad, Ed. I was mad at the whole world because everything I'd tried to do had gone sour. The Allens were mad at the world, too. Maybe that's why I threw in with them."

"You know now why they wanted you?"

Joe thought about it. "Yeah, I guess I do. There wasn't an ounce of real guts between 'em, good as they were with their guns. After I braced 'em for trying to steal my horse, they figured maybe I had guts enough for three."

For a while there was silence inside the cabin. Outside, Dalhart's voice yelled exultantly, "Time's gettin' short, by

God! Another hour an' we'll have a rope around his neck!"

Ed looked at Joe. "Go on, Joe. The time *is* getting short."

Joe's face seemed paler in the dim light. His eyes had a staring, trapped quality. Ed had seen many men who awaited death, so the look was not new to him. He was proud of the steady way Joe's voice spoke, proud of the way the pallor disappeared from his face as he talked.

The germ of an idea was growing in Ed's mind, an idea that might save Joe from the mob outside, but he had to know more about Joe himself. He had to know all of it.

Joe spoke swiftly, and there was a certain reluctant shame in his tone.

— —

He'd bought the supplies in Hobson without any difficulty, and, returning, had picked up the Allens' trail and followed it. He found them eight or ten miles back in the hills, camped beside a small spring, the area around which showed no horse tracks and but few cattle tracks.

Oh, they were a careful pair, all right. They'd erased all sign of the scuffle last night there beside the river. Then they'd ridden toward Hobson, paralleling Joe's tracks but being careful not to cross or cover them. Halfway to Hobson, they'd ridden into the river, and had backtracked in shallow water for several miles. Coming out, they'd picked a rocky dry wash, and thus had reached their campsite without leaving a track save for the ones they wanted Joe to see.

Now they settled down into a routine of eating, sleeping, and standing watch on a high knoll that overlooked the desert and the twisting ribbon of river.

They were days of boredom while Noah was inactive.

Due perhaps to the filthy condition of his shirt, through which Joe's bullet had torn, his wound became infected, and for several days he lay flushed with fever. But when the wound began to heal, when the flush left his face, he began to watch Joe, a certain speculation in his face.

The second week he looked across the fire at Joe one day and said, "That's a hell of a way to wear your gun, Joe. Too high. You got to raise your hand and crook your elbow to get it out. Then, bringing it forward, it's liable to catch on the holster. A guy could get killed wearing his gun thataway."

Joe hitched self-consciously at the gun and belt. Noah grinned his perpetual vacuous grin and said, "Stand up. Loosen it so it hangs about four-five inches lower'n your belt."

Joe let the buckle out several notches. He pushed the gun down until it lay snugly against his thigh. He yanked the gun out, with what he thought a creditable speed.

Noah chuckled. "Too slow." He got up. "Try it again."

Joe did, but before he had the gun clear, Noah's was centered on his middle, hammer back.

Noah chuckled again. "Come on. I'll show you."

Noah cut a thong from the latigo on his saddle and, kneeling, tied Joe's holster to his leg. "Sometimes, if the gun sticks a little, the holster will pull up. Then the whole business binds. The thong holds the holster down, so if you have to yank a little hard, the holster stays put."

He removed Joe's gun and looked at the holster. "Pretty good. It ain't been oiled till it's soft. Never oil a holster, Joe. Soap it. Soap makes the leather slick without softenin' it too much."

He got out a pocket knife and pared Joe's holster away a

little so that the trigger guard was clear. He said, "Make it all one motion. Hand around the grip, finger in the trigger guard first. Then, as you pull, your thumb cocks the hammer. Bring it up and fire the second it's in line."

Joe tried several times. Noah's eyes sparkled. "Keep tryin' for a couple of days. Go on and practice. When you think you're pretty good, come show me."

Joe gave no thought to Noah's reasons for teaching him this fast-draw technique. It was enough that he was. And it helped pass the time.

He practiced for three days. Then he came to Noah, and beat Noah to the draw. Noah's eyebrows raised.

"Fine. I figured you could be good if you tried. But it ain't so much how you get your gun out in a fight as how straight you get the bullet off. Come on. We got plenty of shells. We'll practice a while."

They walked up a bare, dry draw for half a mile. Noah drew a circle in the bank with a stick. "No time for aiming in a fight, Joe. But shootin' from the hip is just like pointing a finger. Try it."

Joe did. The first time, he got one shot out of five in the circle. The second round, he put two inside, close to the center.

Noah tossed him a box of shells. "Practice that a while. Let me know when you can get five out of five in the circle."

Joe was back inside an hour. Noah gave him some more shells. "Now see how fast you can get five in the circle."

Joe went back up the draw a short distance and practiced some more. Between rounds he heard Claude say, "I hope to hell you know what you're doin'. We're packing a couple of thousand in gold. So you teach a hungry kid to draw faster an' shoot straighter than either of us can. Is that good sense?"

Noah chuckled. "I know what I'm doin'."

When Joe came back, Noah said, "The last five in the circle, Joe?"

Joe nodded. Noah murmured, "Keep at it. A man's never good enough for every other man he's likely to meet. So he's got to keep getting better."

"All right."

"And there's another thing. You got to watch a man's eyes. There's always somethin' about 'em that gives him away. Mebbe they narrow a little. I don't know exactly, but it's somethin' you got to learn to recognize like you recognize the rattle of a snake." He stood up. "Watch my eyes now, Joe. See if you know when I make up my mind to draw. The minute you think I have, you draw."

They tried that several times, after which Noah nodded with satisfaction. "You're doing good, Joe. Just remember. Don't ever hesitate. Sometimes a man'll draw on you when there don't seem to be no reason why he should. If you want to stay alive, you'll beat him to it."

Joe looked puzzled, and opened his mouth as though to speak. But he changed his mind. Suppose he had no intention of becoming a gunman? Suppose he had no intention of throwing in with these two outlaws? It wouldn't hurt him to know how to defend himself, would it?

The days passed, and gradually Noah's bullet-bitten side healed. And the time came when Joe woke up in the morning to find the two Allen brothers busy striking camp.

"We've laid around long enough, Joe. We're pullin' out.

I've got kind of fond of you. How'd you like to come?"

Joe shook his head reluctantly. He had to admit that he hated the thought of leaving these two. For one thing, they'd given him confidence by treating him as an equal at first, later with a certain reluctant respect. If he left them, he was back where he started, traveling alone, looking for a job that he might never find. But he said, "I don't want no part of anything the law'll be after me for."

Noah laughed heartily. "We wasn't suggestin' that. Hell, we got enough to travel a while. Maybe go to Arizona for the winter. We ain't figurin' on pullin' no jobs. You stick with us, Joe. We'll live off the country as we go. You can hang onto your two hundred till spring, and then you'll have a better chance of gettin' on steady somewheres. Ain't nobody hirin' cow punchers this time of year."

That clinched it. Joe nodded. He wanted to hang onto his two hundred. Next spring if he could get a steady job at thirty per, it would only take, let's see, ten months to save up the rest. With a steady job and five hundred in the bank, he could send for Molly.

They rode out, heading south. They splashed across the river and were lost in the reaches of high desert.

Joe rode with a lonely, hungry, remembering look in his eyes. He was thinking of Molly. He was thinking that now he almost had it made. Another year—hardly more than a year—and Molly would be his forever.

CHAPTER THIRTEEN

If Joe found it strange that Noah and Claude Allen should head south, he said nothing. But it was strange. They had been fleeing northward from something when he met them, probably the law. Why, then, did they not continue to go north?

Joe found something else about the pair disturbing. Noah's perpetual smile seemed to contain a new ingredient, smugness and satisfaction, as though he had pulled off something. Balancing Noah's smugness was Claude's nervous anxiety, which seemed to have no basis.

But Joe was, if not completely happy, at least satisfied. He had found with the Allens the same acceptance and sense of belonging that he had so valued in Dalhart's employ. And at least the Allens' minds did not have the innate nastiness that Dalhart's had.

The sun baked him, seared his face and hands a deep, smooth brown. He became dusty, and ragged as the Allens were. He shaved seldom, for water was at a premium.

Always Noah kept at him about his gun skill. It became a game of readiness, with Noah likely to say sharply at any instant, "Joe! Behind you!"

And Joe would whirl, hand lancing toward his side, where the smooth-gripped gun snuggled. The gun would clear, and Joe's darting eyes would find the target Noah had selected for him. Usually Joe's bullet found its mark. When it didn't, Noah would say, "You're dead, Joe. You missed him and he got you."

Noah's story was Joe's own story in essence, except that there had been no Ed Mallory to cushion the blows.

Noah and Claude were the sons of a Yankee Army sergeant, caught by the war's end in New Orleans, who saw opportunities for profit in the South's prostration. He had married a mulatto woman, who in the first two years of their marriage had borne him two sons, Noah and Claude. Thereafter he had followed various devious paths to profit, which he found in abundance.

His methods of enriching himself, however, fell under the scrutiny of the local Ku Klux Klan, as did his union with the mulatto. He ignored their repeated warnings. And so one night when Noah was five and Claude four, the Klan rode up and surrounded their isolated mansion.

The house they burned. By its light, on the vast front lawn, they stripped Hugh Allen, tied him to a tree, and lashed him with a bull whip until his back was ribbons. His wife they whipped similarly, and then left both to die, moaning and screaming with agony.

Noah and Claude watched the horror from the concealment of the uncleared brush that surrounded the mansion, and fled in terror before it was quite finished.

Eventually, after wandering an incredible distance, they were taken in by a small farmer deep in the pine woods. Here they learned the meaning of the word work.

Fear they had learned the night the Klan raided their home. Now, from the farmer, they learned to cringe and duck and lie. Ill fed and overworked, they stayed until they were old enough to run again, until Claude was ten and Noah eleven.

A childhood of servility, of invariably losing to adults who were bigger and stronger, did something to them both. And now, grown, neither of them could ever meet a problem directly, but must skirt around it the way a coyote skirts a badger, knowing he cannot win in open conflict, knowing also that a way will be found in slyness and in guile.

They were animals without apparent courage, yet with a certain deadliness in spite of its lack. But one thing they had learned, over the span of years: They had learned to hide their craven spirits behind a mask of toughness. They had learned that courage can be feigned.

Not forever, but for a while.

And the while was enough in Joe's case. He did not discover their cowardice until it was too late. He did not understand Noah's plan until after it had worked.

Eventually, after traveling for nearly a month, they rode into a town called Wilson Creek, in northeastern Arizona.

Joe was tired of his filthy clothes. He was tired of eating like an animal, squatting beside a tiny fire. He was tired of sleeping on the ground. He was weary of the Allens' company, weary of his own solitary thoughts.

Noah's suggestion that they stay in Wilson Creek a few days came as a welcome surprise that he didn't question. He assumed they had passed the place where the Allen brothers were wanted, assumed they were now safe.

In his anticipation, he did not notice Claude's gray-faced fear, his obvious reluctance to enter the town. He gave no thought to Claude's last-minute remembrance, "Hell, I left my knife back where we camped last night. I'm goin' after it. See you in two-three hours."

Joe rode down the street of the town hungrily, yearning for a bed in the hotel, a meal in the restaurant at a table with a clean gingham cloth upon it.

Joe and Noah stabled their horses, and then, lugging a pair of saddlebags each, headed for the town's single hotel, the Union.

Noah dropped a little behind, and if Joe slowed to let him

come abreast, Noah slowed too.

Had Joe been more experienced, more sly himself, he would have searched his mind for Noah's motive. Being young, being inexperienced, he gave it no thought, other than to be faintly irritated and to say, "For Christ's sake, come on! I've been waiting months to soak in a real honest-to-God bathtub."

He scarcely noticed the stone building before him, gave but fleeting attention to the man who lounged before it. He did not even mark the silver star on the man's vest, the gold lettering on the window that read, "Sheriff's Office. Montezuma County."

It therefore came as a complete surprise, this sudden movement that he caught only out of the corner of his eye.

Instinctively his hand flashed to his gun. Instinctively, or as a result of Noah's careful conditioning. Joe did not know that behind him Noah had made a feint toward his gun, did not know that having made his feint, he slipped quickly into the passageway between the sheriff's office and the building next to it.

But the sheriff had seen the feint—from a man he had chased four hundred miles and lost. To the sheriff it was not a feint, but a threat, death whispering to him from the vast, long distances where death lurks.

As in a play, the action unfolded, taking but seconds from the time it began until it was finished. In Joe's mind, Noah's words echoed even as his hand closed on the gun grips: "Sometimes a man'll draw on you when there don't seem to be no reason why he should. If you want to stay alive, you'll beat him to it."

Those thoughts echoed, and then the conditioning took

hold of him. Smoothly, with no waste motion, the gun cleared its stiff, smooth holster, and leveled, hammer back.

Fast. Deadly fast. The sheriff's eyes, puzzled by Noah's disappearance, by this new and unexpected threat, widened almost imperceptibly with amazement at what he saw. Because what he saw was death, staring at him out of the eyes of a kid scarcely eighteen years old.

Cool through a dozen gun fights, he was not cool now. He pulled his trigger frantically, the foolish way a hunter sometimes will when his game is disappearing into the timber.

He pulled it only once. And then Joe's gun was level, centering on his chest, on the silver star that was pinned there.

Joe's eyes saw that star for the first time, and telegraphed their message to his brain. His brain willed his hand to move, so that the bullet would not go where his conditioned reflexes had pointed it.

But the bullet was already on its way out of the gun barrel, and it struck the sheriff somewhere just above the star.

Seconds passed while the street was silent as a tomb; seconds while Joe stared at the man swaying on his feet before him, a man he had never seen before but whom he would see again in a thousand dreams.

The nameless sheriff seemed to jackknife forward, as though his belly hurt him instead of his heart. His hat fell from his head, exposing a thin shock of slate-gray hair. And then he pitched forward so that Joe had to step swiftly aside to avoid him. He lay still, stretched out face downward on the weathered boardwalk.

Sound began in a low murmur along the street, a fearful, low murmur that would grow as outrage grew, that would mount until it was a roar of indignation.

From behind Joe, Noah's voice breathed a shocked "He's dead! You've killed him!"

Joe swiveled his head and looked helplessly at Noah, who had now reappeared. "He drew on me. He fired first. Hell, what was I supposed to do?"

Noah's face was pasty gray. His lips worked, for once without the vapid smile. He croaked, "You done just right. But the town won't think so. We'd better get the hell out of here—fast!"

"But why? It was self-defense."

Noah managed a sour smile. "No such thing as self-defense when the other guy's a lawman. Are you comin', or are you going to stand there jawin' all day?"

They ran for the stable, covering the milling crowd behind them with their threatening guns. They ran crab-wise, and sideways, and always their guns pointed back.

Their own horses were beat. So at gunpoint they forced a trade with the terrified old stableman.

It was wrong, all wrong. And Joe knew it was. But was it not simply a continuation of what had gone before?

They rode out—not at a frantic run, but at a steady lope. For, Noah said, it takes a while before the shock wears away from a town that has been hurt. It takes a while before men can organize, before outrage builds into fury.

Lope and walk, trot and lope again. Spare your horses, for the posse will not spare theirs. To hell with Claude. Let him look out for himself. Let him find you later.

This was life and death, and you either played it

smart or died.

The miles flowed like ribbon beneath the hoofs of their horses. They cared for their mounts, giving no thought to themselves.

Yet danger could not still the workings of Joe's mind, could not deaden his overpowering knowledge that he had been duped.

He said, "This is beginning to fit together. That sheriff knew you, didn't he?"

"No use denying it, Joe. He did."

"Was he the one that had been chasing you and Claude?"

Noah nodded.

"Then why did you deliberately ride into his town?"

Noah was silent, and his eyes would not meet Joe's.

"And what did you do that made him go for his gun?"

"Nothin', Joe. I swear it. He was edgy, maybe. He saw me so damned unexpectedly, I suppose, that his nerves went back on him. Too bad. He sure took you by surprise."

"Yeah. He sure as hell did. Just the way you figured he would. You're a sly bastard, Noah."

"You've got it wrong, Joe." Noah's smile had faded. His eyes were flat and frightened.

"Yeah. It adds up. You wanted that sheriff out of the way, but you couldn't do it yourself. So you sharpened me up the way a man sharpens a knife. And I killed the sheriff for you." He stared at Noah in a way that made Noah's hands begin to tremble. "It'd have been easy for you to make a pass at your gun. You were behind me all the way through town. It irritated me because I was in a hurry. But you weren't in a hurry, were you? Or else you wanted to be a couple of steps behind me."

"You're wrong, Joe. I swear it."

"Goddamn you to hell! I ought to kill you right now." Joe's voice was deadly.

"No, Joe. Don't do it! I won't draw. You'll have to murder me."

Noah kept his hands on the saddle horn. He forged ahead and gave Joe his back.

For a while, anger simmered hot and steady in Joe's mind. But finally it began to fade before his sense of utter futility. He was hooked. No use denying it. Noah had him.

He closed his eyes, but he could not close out the sight of the sheriff, falling. Or of the limp, lifeless way his body had looked lying face downward on the boardwalk.

Joe tried to examine himself, his own character. Perhaps they had been right back in Du Bois. He remembered Ledbetter's words, spoken so long ago: "He'll come to a bad end. He'll end up killing somebody."

And Ledbetter had been right. Joe had killed somebody, somebody he didn't even know and certainly didn't hate.

Joe looked ahead at Noah's back, which was stiff, straining with fear. His lips twisted, but their twisting did not make a smile.

Even Noah distrusted him, feared him. Even Noah did not believe in him enough to know he would not shoot a man in the back.

The hours fled, as Noah and Joe fled, and at last, near nightfall, they heard the shouts of the posse far behind. Noah looked around and grinned, his fear of Joe gone, his mask of courage in place. "We're all right now. Our horses are halfway fresh. Theirs ain't. They've got to stop for night, but we can keep right on travelin'. By morning we'll be so far ahead they'll never catch us."

Joe's thoughts were bitter. No, this posse would never catch them. But every telegraph wire in the Southwest would carry their description. Every lawman, local, state, federal, would be on the lookout for them.

CHAPTER FOURTEEN

Again they traveled south, but they bore eastward now, heading for the great staked plains of Texas, for the Panhandle, where outlaws might find safety among their own kind, among dishonest law officers who ignored the "Wanted" bulletins that came through on the telegraph and in the mail.

Joe was silent, sour, moody, and withdrawn. Only once in the next three days did he speak to Noah, and then it was to ask, "I might as well know the name of the man I killed. What was it?"

"Nordley. James Nordley."

Joe glanced at Noah sharply. What boy growing to manhood failed to learn that name? It stood with the names Holliday and Masterson, Hickok and Earp. Joe said, "You're lying."

"No, I'm not. I swear it, Joe. You're good—fast enough maybe to beat the best. Nordley might have slowed a little, but he hadn't slowed much."

"And that was *the* James Nordley? Not another one with the same name?"

"It was James Nordley, all right. He got off the first shot, didn't he?"

Joe's face flushed. "Damn you, you knew what would

happen. I haven't got a chance of finding a cow-punching job now. I haven't the chance of a snowball in hell of finding any kind of job. All right, let's have it. What's in that twisted, slimy mind of yours? What're you planning to do?"

Something sparkled in Noah's eyes. "We can be rich, Joe. We can all be rich as nabobs. I figured a three-man gang, but it's better this way. I can get ahold of Claude. We always agreed that if we got separated, we'd meet in Santa Fe. I'll write him there and tell him where we are."

"And?"

"He wasn't in on Nordley's killin', and Nordley was the only one who saw him the night we robbed the Wilson Creek Bank. Claude's in the clear except for Nordley's description. All he's got to do is shave off his mustache."

"Then what?"

"Why, you and me can pull the jobs, Joe. Claude can bring us grub and news while we're holed up afterward."

"Got it all figured out, haven't you?"

"Sure, Joe. Sure I have."

"Except for one thing." Joe's eyes flared angrily. "I'm out. I'm through."

Noah grinned his meaningless grin. "That's up to you. But I can tell you how it'll be. You find a job, out on some ranch where they're busy with work and haven't time to worry about anything but that work. Fine. But how long before some drifter comes riding in and recognizes you from your description? How long before the local sheriff, who sure as hell keeps his eyes on strangers and drifters, sees you and recognizes you himself? You're a marked man, Joe, whether you realize it or not. You're the man who killed James Nordley. It puts you in a class by yourself. The law's after you because Nordley was a lawman and a good one. And that ain't all. Every two-bit gun-slinger in the Southwest will be wondering how fast you are. They'll be wondering if you've got the guts to back up your speed with a gun. Some of them will try to find out."

Joe looked at him. Noah's face was flushed, oily with sweat and unholy enthusiasm. Joe had often wondered what Noah's eyes reminded him of. Now he knew. They were like a boar's eyes, hidden in their folds of fatty flesh. They looked out with feral hunger, as though everything they looked upon were only food for a voracious appetite. The man was crafty, sly, merciless. His courage, which Joe knew existed, was the courage of desperation, to be used only when all else failed.

He would fawn and cringe, would accept insult with his unchanging smile to avoid a fight, even when he might have won. And yet, cornered, he would probably surprise everybody who knew him, would probably surprise even himself. Cornered, he might at last fully realize his own capabilities, which in the thirty-odd years of his life he had not yet done.

Joe looked away, somehow repelled at the evil that dwelt in Noah Allen. Yet the man's face remained in his mind, shaggy and shapeless, distinguished only by the feral eyes, the smiling, loose-lipped mouth, the straight, almost patrician nose.

Even Joe, inexperienced though he was, could realize that this was a crossroads, perhaps the most important crossroads of his life. Upon his decision now hinged his future, his life or death.

And yet, what else was there? Noah had called the turn,

had predicted with obvious accuracy what would happen to Joe if he went out and took a cow-punching job. And even Joe could predict what would happen if he tried to find a job in town.

Joe's mind rebelled. He said, "No squirrel cage for me. I've got a couple of hundred. I'll lay low down in the Panhandle until it's gone. Maybe by then the heat will be off."

Noah shrugged. "Suit yourself. But when your money's gone, when you're ready to face reality in your mind, I'll be around."

That night they rode into a town called Gila. It was a typical Spanish town, built of adobe. Fall rains had turned its dusty streets to mud. Joe looked at Noah. "This is it. If I never see your scheming face again it'll be too soon."

Noah smiled benignly. "You'll see me. You'll want to see me."

Joe rode away, leaving Noah looking after him.

He put his horse up at a corral near the edge of town. Then he found a small Mexican restaurant and filled his hungry belly with hot Mexican food.

After that he wandered from one end of the town to the other, its damp stink in his nostrils, its noise in his ears. Hogs squealed, scuffling in the main street for an ear of corn previously undiscovered. Voices rose in argument, in liquid song, in drunken laughter.

Dusk crept, gray and still, across the town. Joe thought of Molly, and Ed Mallory, and homesickness gripped his mind. He did then what Noah Allen had perhaps expected him to do. He did what any lonely kid in a strange town might do. He found a saloon, a cantina.

Joe was not used to drinking, though he had done some

at Dalhart's urging over the past few years. In fiery tequila, he found that his loneliness lessened, his feeling of hopelessness disappeared.

He drank half a bottle of tequila, and with his head reeling got up to leave, to search out a room in which to sleep.

He stepped onto the gallery before the adobe saloon. Beside the door, an idler wrapped in a serape strummed a guitar, his hat pulled low over his eyes.

The night was cool, pleasant. Joe Redenko started down the walk, looking for a hotel, any place in which to sleep.

His reflexes slowed by liquor, his alertness stilled, he tripped on a cord stretched between the tie rail and the dark, narrow alleyway. And then they were on him, pinning him face down in the mud.

A gun barrel crashed against the back of his head. Still he struggled, and down it came again. Blackness enveloped him.

When he came to, he lay where he had fallen. Blood was a wetness in his hair, and it had dried in a thin crust on the back of his neck. But his gun was gone, and so were the saddlebags he had carried slung over his shoulder. His pockets were turned inside out.

He struggled to his feet, and his head seemed to explode with pain. White light seared his eyeballs. Reeling, he staggered into the alley, and collapsed upon a heap of straw.

Unconsciousness clutched at his mind. He had but one thought before it claimed him. There was no choice now. Within days the news would be out and he would be notorious, wanted for the murder of James Nordley. He was broke, and he hadn't even a gun. Honest jobs were denied him. But one course remained open. Tomorrow he would seek out Noah Allen, as Noah had predicted.

———

He stared across at Ed Mallory, whose form was now but a shadowy blur in the darkening cabin. He, said, "I went to Noah the next morning, and I stayed with him and Claude until they were dead." He stopped, his face suddenly faintly puzzled. "Funny. They used me, but even so, I've got the feeling they liked me. I even wonder sometimes if Noah wasn't sorry about the way he'd suckered me in."

"Tell me about it, Joe." Ed's voice was expressionless, neither approving nor disapproving. Nor was it merely curious. Ed had to know about Joe. He had to know if the things Joe had done with the Allens had changed him. He had to know for Molly's sake, for Joe's, for his own.

He listened as Joe's voice went on, hurried, a little frantic now. For the time was short, reduced to but little more than half an hour.

———

Noah staked him and bought him another gun, a new Colt's patent .44. Nor did Noah display resentment that Joe had left him and come crawling back. He was his old self, suppressing whatever feelings he might have had to attain the end he wanted.

They contacted Claude, and waited in Gila until he arrived. Thereafter, they worked a carefully thought-out system.

Claude went ahead and picked the jobs. When he had them all sized up, he came back, and between the three they planned until they had it perfect, even to their escape route and the hiding place where they'd stay until the pursuit died down.

Four jobs a year. The first year it was a bank, a Wells-Fargo gold shipment, an isolated roadhouse, a wealthy rancher returning from Kansas City with the proceeds of his herd in cash.

Four jobs a year, and it all went off like clockwork, with Joe insisting that there be no killings.

There were none. Yet their notoriety spread far and wide. Since they killed no witnesses, there was always someone to spread the word. "It was the Allen gang, Noah and that kid that gunned Nordley. The other Allen wasn't with 'em, but he's mixed up in it somewheres, providin' he ain't already dead."

Four jobs the first year, and always a hiding place when the job was done, a hiding place stocked with provisions and liquor, and with Claude to bring them news so that they'd know when pursuit was abandoned.

Four jobs, and then a fifth, perhaps the most dangerous yet: the Wells-Fargo bank at Monument, Arizona.

Joe was nineteen that fall, but he looked twenty-five. He still took Noah's orders, but only because he wished to issue none himself. He was still reluctant, still unwilling. And still, in his lonely moments, he dreamed of Molly and of all that might have been.

His lonely moments were many, for all that he had attained was a maturity that made acceptance and approval less necessary to him. He no longer needed Claude and Noah, being increasingly sufficient unto himself. He stayed with them because he still knew of nothing else to do. Yet in staying he found little companionship, little assuagement of the eternal loneliness that plagued him.

He welcomed, therefore, the sight of their hiding place when the job at Monument was done, the sight of a woman in the lonely yard, hanging clothes on a line stretched between two poles.

He turned and looked questioningly at Noah, who was still shaky from the robbery. It had not gone well and a man had been killed.

Noah said, "This was all we could find. They're hard up and willing to take us in if we'll pay the price."

Joe shrugged, his eyes on the woman. "It's all right with me. I'll have somebody to talk to besides you."

"Be damned sure that's all you do—talk. Start messin' with that girl and we'll be fresh out of a place to stay."

Girl! She wasn't married, then. Joe felt his blood stir as they rode closer, as he saw that she was pretty, too.

He caught Noah watching him nervously, almost fearfully, and realized two things very suddenly. One was that he hated Noah, had hated him for a long time. The second was that Noah was afraid of him.

Probably with good cause, too. Joe suspected that, among other things, Noah had been responsible for that robbery and slugging back in Gila. He suspected as well that the killing in Monument had been unnecessary, suspected that it had been a bit of pure viciousness on Noah's part. Noah had told him the guard went for his gun, but Joe didn't believe it.

Fearing Joe, perhaps Noah had let worry gnaw at him until he became as ill-tempered as Joe was himself. Perhaps he had shot the guard when the person he really wanted to shoot was Joe.

Joe looked away from Noah's face. The puzzlement and

hurt had gone from Joe's moody eyes in the last year, to be replaced by a coldness that never left them. Joe's face was leaner too, darker. There were lines of disillusionment and bitterness around his eyes.

Noah had told him often, "Damn it, you live inside yourself too much. You let your troubles pile up in your mind like water behind a dam. Let loose once in a while. Get drunk, or get yourself a woman. Loosen up and let your goddamn troubles go. If you don't, you're going to go haywire."

Joe shook his head savagely as though to clear these thoughts away. He looked down at the girl before them.

She was small, and dressed in a full skirt that just missed the ground. Above the waist she wore a boy's shirt, open at the throat. Every time she reached up to pin a garment to the line, her breasts pushed against the shirt in a way that made Joe's blood pound.

Her hair was dark, loosely caught in a bun at the nape of her neck, a bun from which tendrils escaped in damp confusion. There were beads of perspiration on her upper lip, and her eyes were dark and sullen as she looked up.

First she looked at Noah, and immediately afterward she buttoned another button on her shirt. Joe chuckled and Noah flushed. Then she looked at Joe.

"You're the two that're going to hide out here, I suppose."

Joe nodded. His mouth was solemn, but there was a flicker of interest in his eyes, and the remnants of his amusement at the way she'd put Noah in his place.

The girl said irritably, "Well, don't sit there gawking. Haven't you ever seen a girl before?"

Noah asked, "Where's your old man?"

She tossed her head toward the house, then turned back to her work and thereafter ignored their presence.

Joe reined over to the house and dismounted. Noah, with a last look at the girl's hips, followed him.

Noah started to knock on the door, but it opened before he could. Framed in it stood a middle-aged man, partly bald, with thin, graying hair. The impression he gave Joe was one of helplessness, of vagueness.

Noah said, "I'm Noah Allen. This is Joe Redenko. My brother said he'd fixed it so we could stay here a while."

"Of course. Of course. Come in, gentlemen."

Joe went in. Noah went back to his horse and removed his saddlebags. He carried them inside and brought forth a handful of gold. He counted out three hundred dollars onto the table. "There's half. You get the other half when we leave. All right?"

"Yes. That's all right." The man gathered up the gold coins hurriedly.

The door opened and the girl came in, carrying the empty tub in which she had carried out her clean clothes. She set it down and crossed to her father. "I'll take that, Dad. You won't need it. They won't let you go to town as long as they're here." Her voice was firm, but surprisingly gentle.

She turned to Joe, dislike coming into her face. "You can sleep in the stable loft. There's still a little hay up there left over from last winter. But I'll ask you not to smoke up there."

Noah licked his lips, his eyes steady on the girl. Joe said, "Come on, Noah."

The girl followed them out. Noah led his horse away, but the girl stopped Joe with a glance. "Your partner brought supplies for you when he made the arrangements for you to stay. There's a lot of whisky. I . . ." She swallowed and went on determinedly: "Please don't give any of it to my father. It's his weakness. It's the reason we have to harbor outlaws to live."

Joe felt mildly irritated. She could offer an insult and ask a favor in the same breath, all the while looking at him as though he had just crawled out from under a flat rock. He started to say, "You'll have to ask me nicer than that," but he stopped himself. Noah would have said that, his eyes suggesting, his mouth twisted into a leer.

Joe said, "All right. I'll do the best I can." And he followed Noah toward the stable.

— —

From Noah, later, Joe learned a little about the girl.

Her name was Evelyn Morse, and her father called her Eve. She was another of life's prisoners, as Joe was, in that she could not leave her father, who was a hopeless, incurable drunk.

So she had moved him out here, far enough away from town and its liquor supply so that it was a long day's ride to get there. She'd sold their house in town and bought this abandoned ranch.

It had helped, too. Except that the money left over had run out sooner than she had expected.

Near to desperation, because going broke out here meant a return to town and her father's return to sodden drunkenness, she had listened from necessity to Claude's proposal that she hide his brother and his brother's partner in crime.

Claude offered her six hundred dollars, which, she said, would last her nearly two years. By that time, she hoped her father might be cured.

Joe came up in back of the house one day to wash for dinner and accidentally overheard a conversation between Eve and her father, a conversation that revealed her personal feelings in the matter.

He heard her father's voice: "Eve, what are you doing with that gun? Put it away."

"I'm putting it away—here in the drawer in the kitchen where it'll be handy."

"Handy for what? What are you afraid of?"

Her voice had an exasperated quality. "I'm afraid of those two men. I made a mistake in agreeing to let them stay here, and now I don't know how to get rid of them."

"They're not bothering us. Why get rid of them?"

"Because they're killers, Pa. They're cold-blooded and without decency. The older one looks at me like an animal, and the young one is cold as ice. They give me the chills."

Concern was noticeable in her father's voice. "You just put that gun away and forget you've got it. Those two are as wary as wild animals. They live by their guns. What chance would you have and what good would that gun do you against them? You'd never catch either of them off guard."

"Then what can we do?"

"Let them alone. Don't talk to them. Don't allow yourself to be alone with either of them. Above all, don't ever pull that gun on them. It'd be like poking a tiger with a stick."

Joe's face was flaming. His eyes were bright with anger. He turned and walked carefully and silently away from the house, only pausing when he was some distance from it.

After a few moments, however, his anger and resentment

began to leave. Why, after all, should he resent such a frank appraisal from the girl? Why? She'd made it on the basis of what she saw, at least, not on the basis of who Joe's parents were. She'd seen only what was there to be seen: in Noah, a savage hunger; in Joe, coldness.

Joe's anger ebbed, but when it was gone it left emptiness behind.

CHAPTER FIFTEEN

The days were days of boredom and inactivity for Noah and Joe. Morse had driven their horses away, to graze with a small band of his own, far back in the hills. It would not do, he said, to have their horses near the house, where a chance visitor might see them and where they might be identified. He was protecting himself and his daughter, Joe knew, probably at the daughter's suggestion.

Noah protested, but Joe told Morse to go ahead anyway.

He puzzled himself these days. He had lost his old anxiety about being caught. Now it seemed he no longer particularly cared. Could being caught be worse than a lifetime of this, stealing money you didn't want from people who did? Risking your life and, worse, risking other lives in an occupation you hated?

Then Noah began to drink. When they went in to supper the evening of the eighth day, he was tipsy enough to stagger against the table and nearly upset it.

Morse looked at Noah and licked his lips. He swallowed a couple of times, and then began to cough. Joe looked at the man's hands and saw that they were trembling.

Evelyn's face was pale as she served the meal. She kept

looking anxiously at her father, then at Noah, then in a kind of desperation at Joe.

And Noah, as though his restraint were weakened by the liquor he had consumed, kept his eyes on Evelyn. Once, when she passed him, he rubbed her leg with his hand.

She started and moved away, otherwise ignoring him. But the fear in her eyes was doubled, her pallor increased. And thereafter she avoided Noah's side of the table.

Morse didn't eat much. He kept looking at Noah, the way a spaniel looks at a man who is eating. His eyes begged, but Noah only grinned his meaningless grin.

So Morse turned his eyes to Joe, and when Joe went out, he followed and caught timidly at his sleeve. Morse cleared his throat, and his words tumbled out: "Been a long time since I've been to town. Man gets so he misses a little nip once in a while. You know, my daughter won't let me keep it around here. I used to hide out a pint once in a while, but she always found them. Awful the way women boss a man around, ain't it? I don't suppose you boys have got a bottle in your stuff somewhere, have you? Reckon you could spare a man a little nip?"

Joe shook his head. "Your daughter said no. Sorry."

"Oh, my daughter said no, did she? Now, who the hell does she think she is?"

Joe wanted to say, "Maybe the one who's holding you together." But he didn't. Morse couldn't help himself any more than Joe could, any more than Evelyn could. They were all trapped, perhaps by the weakness inside them, perhaps by circumstances, perhaps by a combination of both.

They had a lamp and a table in the lower part of the stable. Usually they played cards or checkers after supper until bedtime came. But tonight Noah was too drunk to play, and besides, Joe suddenly couldn't stand the sight of him. So he went outside.

It was cool and pleasant. He went over and climbed up on the corral fence.

He could see into the kitchen from here. He could see Eve moving around, clearing off the supper table, washing the dishes. She was clean and crisp-looking, fresh even after a day of work, a change from the jaded, weary, cynical saloon women who had been Joe's only feminine companions since leaving Du Bois.

He found himself wondering what it would be like to hold her in his arms, to nuzzle the soft hollow of her throat, to feel her warmth and softness against him.

His excitement grew, and this was elemental, the age-old desire of a man for a woman. Yet in Joe tonight there was something else, something that would forbid any attempt to fulfill his desire. It was a need for something deeper than mere physical satisfaction. It was a need for love, so that the two might be combined into fulfillment comparable to that which he had known with Molly.

Molly. Thinking of her brought a wave of bitter loneliness to his mind. He stared at the stars, and tried to remember each line of her face, each expression her eyes had held as she looked at him.

He remembered the Saturday nights they'd spent on the island, the dreams they'd had and talked about, dreams of a lifetime together.

Joe's face twisted and he realized how tense he was. He forced himself to relax, and built a smoke. He lighted it as Eve came to the door to empty the dishpan.

She saw the flare and came toward him. "Have you seen my father?"

"No." He was thinking, Maybe I could stay here. Maybe after a while she'll change her mind about me. Hell, she needs a man. She can't manage her father forever without help.

But it wouldn't work, and he knew it wouldn't. Noah wouldn't let him go. If Joe stayed, it wouldn't be a week before the law rode into the yard, tipped off by Noah.

Eve said, "Maybe he's in the stable with your friend."

Joe shook his head. "No. I just came from there."

"You didn't . . ."

"Give him a bottle? No. He asked me, but I refused."

"Do you think your friend . . ."

"I doubt it. Stop worrying. Your father's a grown man."

She made a small, bitter laugh. "Is a man responsible who can't control his own destiny?"

Joe looked at her sharply in the dim light. Her face was a pale oval, its expression hidden.

She murmured, not looking at him, "Would you help me with him if I find him? I suppose he's got into your things. I imagine he's stolen a bottle from you. Right now he's probably lying out in the brush somewhere, dead to the world. He's too heavy for me when he's like that. And I don't like to leave him out all night."

"Sure. I'll help you look for him." Joe jumped down from the corral fence.

He followed her as she moved away into the darkness. Over her shoulder she said wearily and with a touch of unease in her voice, "There are several places he goes when he has some whisky. I know them as well as I know him."

For some reason, which he did not immediately understand, Evelyn had a capacity for irritating him. For one thing, her judgments seemed too abrupt and too harsh. For another, Joe's own mind kept comparing himself with Morse, his own problem with Morse's seemingly unrelated one. He had a feeling that Eve was making a similar comparison.

And he had to admit there was justice in that comparison. Morse was a drunk through personal weakness, through his failure to exert enough strength to break free. Joe was a criminal through a like weakness and lack of strength. Perhaps Morse wanted to be a drunk no more than Joe wanted to be a criminal. Yet both of them were drifting, lacking the strength to change.

He searched his mind for relief from the unwelcome admission, and realized that a difference did exist. The habit of surrender to weakness was strong in Morse, perhaps too strong to resist. In Joe it was not. Joe was young. He could yet break free.

A chance would come. He must be ready to recognize it, to seize it when it came.

He halted, bumping against Eve, who had stopped and knelt down. He saw a dim shape lying stretched out on the ground beside her. "Here he is," she said bitterly. "Dead to the world. Can you carry him to the house for me?"

"Sure." Joe stooped and picked the man up. Morse was not heavy. Joe followed the girl again, returning toward the house. He carried Morse in and dumped him on the bed.

"Thank you."

"Sure." He thought he detected more softness in Eve than he had seen before, as though tonight she needed strength, and, in the way of woman, turned to a man for it.

He thought, too, that perhaps tonight he could make love to her if he tried. But her harsh appraisal of him was too fresh in his mind and he didn't try. He turned and went out.

Noah was playing solitaire at the table. He looked up at Joe. His face was slack with liquor, but his eyes were sharp and filled with envy. "You didn't waste no time, did you?"

"What the hell are you talking about?"

"You know what I'm talking about. You an' that girl. I saw you head out into the brush with her. How—"

"Shut up!" Fury flared in Joe, as it had done long ago in the face of Dalhart's insinuations.

Noah said, his eyes burning, "Don't use that tone on me! You gave her old man a bottle, didn't you? To get him out of the way. Then you took out into the brush with the girl. I thought I told you to let her alone."

Joe controlled himself with difficulty, and climbed to the stable loft. But he didn't sleep. In spite of himself, he kept thinking of Eve Morse, thinking that if he had tried, perhaps he could have made love to her. And, even knowing it would have been unfair, he wished he had tried.

Who thinks of fairness when he desperately wants a woman? Joe ridiculed himself in his mind. The world was a jungle, a dog-eat-dog existence where a man must either take the first bite or give it.

Then why hadn't he played it that way? Was it because of Molly? Or was it because some part of him refused to accept Noah's bitter philosophy?

He didn't know. And at last he went to sleep.

He wasn't sure for a moment exactly what it was that awakened him. He lay very still in his bed of dry hay, listening, tense, ready to spring into action at the first indication of danger.

He heard nothing. He looked around for Noah, but in the blackness of the loft he could see nothing. He listened for Noah's breathing, but could hear no sound.

Uneasiness touched him vaguely.

Then he heard again the sound that must have wakened him, faint but recognizable. The sound was that of a woman's scream, muffled by a hand clamped over her mouth.

Immediately Joe was on his feet. He stopped and pulled on his boots. He scooped up his gun and belt and swung down from the loft, dropping the last three feet to the ground.

Outside the stable he halted again, listening intently, trying to place the location of the sound.

And he heard her cry again, this time more moan than scream.

The sound made him furious. Careless of noise, unheeding in his rage, he ran in its direction.

His voice made low, cursing sounds that ended in a high yell. "Noah! You son-of-a-bitch, I'm comin' after you. Turn her loose and watch yourself!"

He heard Noah's sharp grunt of exertion, the scrambling sound that Eve made in getting away. Then there was silence, a short silence followed by Eve's hysterical cry: "He's got his gun! Look out!"

Joe heard his own voice, laughing. "I want him to have it."

Her cry had been very near to him, and he halted abruptly.

Near silence lay like a blanket over the land. The peaks behind the house made a blacker silhouette against a black sky. Wind sighed through the brush, and water in the stream made a faint, continuous, roaring sound. A twig snapped, and Joe's body tensed as he turned to face the sound.

He kicked a brush clump, and leaped away. Noah's gun flared, the bullet cutting with deadly accuracy through the brush clump Joe had stirred with his foot.

But Joe knew now where Noah was. He went forward, slipping along like a cat in pursuit of a sparrow.

Anger grew in him as a fire grows in a dry forest, and fuel was added to it continually in the form of Eve Morse's hurt whimpering, coming faintly to him from Noah's right, where she now crouched.

The past and the present became, in Joe's outraged mind, one and the same, with Noah Allen blending somehow in his thoughts with Jake Dalhart. To Joe, Eve became Molly, brutally violated, and he went a little mad.

Caution fled before his outrage. His feet, heedless in their direct path, made sounds on the twig-littered ground. Again Noah's gun flared, closer now, its noise a roar in Joe's ears.

The bullet burned lightly along the muscles of his left arm.

For the barest fraction of a second, shock held him immobile. Then his right hand flashed with its old instinctive speed to the gun at his side.

Even before pain began in his wounded arm, his gun was level, its hammer back. Unreal was its feel, bucking up in his hand. But the bullets went true, the first, the second, the third.

The first smashed Noah's right wrist. The second, bearing a little more to the right, seared a furrow along his side. The third took him straight through his heart.

And then the night was quiet, save for Joe's harsh breathing, for the slight sound his gun made slipping back into its holster.

Eve Morse got to her feet in terror and fled. She gave no thanks to Joe for saving her further indignity. To Eve it must have been simple. Two savage animals had fought over her, and one had died. But the victor remained, and she fled from him with as much terror as she would have fled from the vanquished.

Partly dazed, Joe heard her go, heard the door of the house slam shut. He even heard the bar drop, so furiously did she slam it into place.

Joe said, "Noah?" expecting no answer, yet compelled to say it anyway.

There was no sound. Joe moved, half afraid, toward the spot where he knew Noah's body lay. His foot touched it, soft and yielding, and he stepped back. Forcing himself, he knelt and put a hand on Noah's chest.

There was no rise and fall of breathing, no steady heartbeat. There was nothing. But when Joe's hand came away, it was wet with blood. He wiped it on his pants with something akin to revulsion. His face contorted in the darkness. His eyes burned.

Weep for this—this yielding clay so limp and lifeless on the ground? Weep because evil had died, because he had found at last, a way to break free of that evil?

No. Weep for the boy, now man-grown, who had killed a second time. Weep because, having killed this second time, he must go on to a third killing, and a fourth—because the evil that he had thought was Noah still had him, even though Noah was dead.

Invisible in the darkness, his face underwent a subtle change. It grew hard and still, and a little more of the dwindling warmth went out of his eyes.

He turned and walked back toward the house. He went into the stable and lighted a coal-oil lantern. Carrying it and a shovel, he returned to Noah's body. He began to dig a grave, ignoring the pain in his arm and the slowly seeping blood that had not yet clotted enough to close the wound.

CHAPTER SIXTEEN

Now he was free—free of the shackles Noah had placed upon him. But even as he thought it, he knew it wasn't true. There was still Claude, who would live for vengeance. There was still the ghost of James Nordley to haunt him. There was still the life he had led with Noah, the crimes chalked against him.

The likeness of Molly Ledbetter began to fade from his mind. This morning, with Noah's grave covered over, with the dawn beginning to gray the eastern horizon, with his eyes red from strain and lack of sleep, Joe tried to call up her image to his mind, and failed.

He lifted his eyes toward the sky, the way he had seen Ed do, and silently asked a God in whom he only half believed if there were any way a man could free himself from his past, from his past's mistakes.

He received no answer, and indeed had expected none.

The door of the house opened, and Eve Morse stood

framed in it, looking across the yard toward the place where he sat, head down now between his hands. She hesitated, then came toward him.

He looked up, and saw her not as a woman he desired, but as all the thing's a woman represents to a man, complex and intermingled. She was his mother, for whose love he had longed as a boy. She was Molly, whose image was now so elusive, both as a woman he loved and as a little girl who gave him sympathy and understanding.

He longed to bury his face in Eve's breasts, to be comforted, but he made no move.

She was pale, still touched by the shock and horror of the night. "I didn't thank you for what you did."

"No need for thanks."

Perhaps she saw the torment in this man she had thought a killer. Perhaps she realized at last that she had misjudged him. She said quickly, "Breakfast is ready. Father's too sick to eat. I hope you won't make me eat alone."

Joe got to his feet and followed her to the house.

Morse was leaving as they entered. His face was gray. A few moments later, Joe heard him retching outside the house. He looked at Eve and saw how the sound twisted her face.

Joe sat down at the table, and Eve sat across from him. It could be like this, Joe thought. He could stay here. Perhaps Eve would not love him, could never love him, but she would marry him because he was a man and because she desperately needed one.

Claude would come, but Claude could be killed. Something shrank within him at the thought. If he killed again, there would be no end to it. He would go on and on, finding the solution to whatever difficulties beset him in killing.

Eve asked in a low voice, "What will you do now? His brother will come sooner or later."

"I know he will." Decision was reached in Joe's mind at last. "But I won't be here. This is my chance to get clear of them. I'm going to take it."

Fear touched her instantly. Joe saw it, and said, "Don't worry. Tell him I killed Noah and took the money with me. He won't waste any time here. He'll get on my trail."

Her mouth, full and red and trying to smile, opened as though to speak, but closed with the words unuttered.

Joe got up and went outside. First he smashed what whisky bottles were left against a rock. Then he placed all the gold, Noah's and Claude's and his own, in a single pair of saddlebags. Leading a spare horse to pack, and riding one of Morse's, he rode up to the door of the house.

"I'm going," he told Eve, and handed her down the three hundred dollars agreed upon. "Tell Claude I rode north. Tell him I'm headed for Montana."

"And you'll go somewhere else?"

"No. I'll head for Montana, all right."

"Then I'll tell him you went south."

He glared at her angrily. "Don't be a fool! Do you know what he'd do if he didn't pick up my trail within a hundred miles or so? He'd come back here. Only this time I wouldn't be here to help."

He saw that he had frightened her, and was satisfied. Now she'd do as he asked. He said, "Good-by. Good luck."

Her eyes held him briefly, asking yet not asking that he stay. He turned his back deliberately and rode away.

For a while, her image remained in his mind, but gradually, as he rode, it faded. Eve Morse became a part of the past, along with Nordley and Noah. And Joe Redenko fled from his past as quickly as his horse would carry him.

It began as a feeling, a vague kind of uneasiness that plagued him whenever he rode skylined along a ridgetop, whenever he camped in a valley surrounded by higher ground.

It began as nervousness, with an inability to sleep soundly at night.

And he knew, at last, that Claude was on his trail.

He knew that Claude watched him at night from the high ground that overlooked his camp. He knew that Claude waited for a chance to put a bullet into him without showing himself, a chance that must surely come.

There would be no warning, Joe knew. Just the terrible shock of the bullet, and afterward the sound of the report, if death did not come too soon.

A month ago, a year ago, he would have told himself he didn't care. Let death come, and with it release from the squirrel cage. But now it was different. He had beaten fate, or thought he had. He had found a turnoff, and had taken it. Now he was damned if a gutless little man with a dry-gulcher's heart was going to take it from him.

To make sure, he backtracked in the early predawn hours, and saw the evidence of Claude's presence with his own eyes—a burned-out fire, the tracks of a single horse over-lying his own.

Ahead, there were ravines and canyons to be crossed, many of them choked with cedar. There were defiles to be threaded, littered with boulders that would hide a man in ambush.

Joe rode with his rifle across his thighs, with his eyes alert, his mouth tightened. He rode with his right hand never far from the gun at his side.

But at night he slept not at all. Dozing, he would start at the sound of a night bird alighting on a nearby tree. A barking coyote a mile away would bring Joe to his elbow, gazing intently into the surrounding darkness.

Claude wanted the gold. But most of all he wanted Joe Redenko dead.

Claude was sleeping soundly, even tonight, up there somewhere in the surrounding buttes. In the morning Claude would wake, would gaze out across the vast desert until he picked up the vaporous dust trail that Joe made. After that, Claude would have a leisurely breakfast, and would go on, not hurrying, patient as Job.

And Joe would go on, spending his wakeful nights, spending with them his waning strength.

The time would come, and Claude must have known it, when Joe's alertness would be drugged by weariness, when his conditioned body and right hand would be slowed by lethargy and fatigue.

Then Claude would move. Then he would ride ahead and select his ambush.

Perhaps he would fail the first time, for Joe traveled no defined trail. Perhaps he would fail a dozen times. But sooner or later Joe would ride past Claude's ambush and Claude's finger would tighten upon his trigger.

Deliberately Joe tried to defeat Claude's plan. First came sleep. He made himself relax, bedded in a spot a quarter mile from where he was camped, and to which he'd creep after full dark had settled down.

He made himself relax, and his weary body fell into the deepest kind of sleep. Joe found that the human mind contains a marvelous waking mechanism. He discovered that all he had to do, before dropping off, was to impress upon his own mind by repetition that he must awake an hour before dawn.

And he always did. Thereupon he would creep back to his campsite and roll himself in his blankets. The first light of day would find him tossing uncomfortably, as though he had spent the entire night there.

His strength and alertness returned. But he was careful to conceal that fact. He let himself droop and doze in the saddle during the day. He dragged himself around his camp at night, a picture of dejection and fatigue, but smiling to himself all the while, and glancing unobtrusively around at the surrounding countryside.

Yet even while Joe strove desperately to preserve his life, he questioned its course for the first time since leaving Eve Morse. He might kill Claude; he must kill Claude, or be killed himself. But in doing so, he would probably discover that he had, in reality, found no escape at all.

Defeatism assailed him. It would always be the same, he told himself. He would always be forced to kill to preserve his own life. Later, perhaps, there would be other reasons for killing—compelling reasons that would seem as logical and necessary as this present one.

So he shrugged, and built himself a shell, a wall against his thoughts. A certain fatalism took possession of him, and he surrendered himself to his destiny, whatever it might be.

He crossed southern Utah along much the same path he

had previously followed with Noah, but he detoured widely around the town of Wilson Creek, wondering if Claude would ride in and inform the new sheriff that Nordley's killer was in the county.

Apparently, however, Claude wanted Joe for himself, for no posse's dust cloud rose on the horizon, and Joe passed the town and left Montezuma County in safety.

Still riding northward, he crossed the Colorado with many a longing look to the east, with many a homesick thought about Du Bois and Ed Mallory and Molly.

They'd hardly recognize him in Du Bois now, but they'd all like to see him, because he was living proof that their predictions had come true.

On the high slopes, on the rolling top of the plateau, the brush turned orange, and quaking aspen turned brilliant yellow. The deer Joe saw were gray and sleek, having shed their summer's brown. The antlers of the bucks gleamed gray-brown, their growth stopped, the velvet worn away on the low-hanging branches of the cedars and piñon pine.

Joe skirted the plateau, though climbing it and cutting across would have been easier. For even Joe could not stay forever alert traveling through country in which every tree was a potential ambush.

Tired of the game, he tried to bait Claude, and deliberately gave him two or three perfect opportunities for ambush each day. But no shot came.

It was a terrible strain, this waiting for a shot that never came. Claude was counting on that strain to break Joe. And when Joe was broken, Claude's work would become easy.

Joe tried to reason as Claude would reason. He knew that he looked exhausted, from fear and lack of sleep. But

Claude was the cautious one. He'd want to be sure. He'd want to test Joe.

Or would he figure that Joe expected a test, and, expecting it, would be unprepared if Claude failed to provide it?

Was Claude's mind that devious, or was Joe giving him too much credit? He decided he was. But he had to be sure.

They crossed the Colorado border and entered Wyoming. They put the low mountains of southwestern Wyoming behind, and dropped down to the rolling sagebrush plains.

And then one day Joe deliberately pointed himself toward a low escarpment on the horizon, toward a rocky defile that led upward toward its top.

He was a picture of desperation by now. He had not shaved for more than two weeks. His clothing was ragged, incredibly filthy. He walked in a kind of exhausted shuffle, and rode with his head swiveling from side to side while his bloodshot eyes ranged the wide horizon.

Approaching the defile, with the rocky escarpment looming above him, Joe experienced a prickling on the back of his neck. Did Claude, lurking up there, feel it too? Did he suspect that the defile was Joe's trap, as well as his own?

Joe shook his head, suddenly not caring particularly. He wanted this game to be over, for it had taken too great a toll.

The defile lay ahead, strewn with rocks the size of a horse that had broken off from the top and rolled here to the bottom. The footing was rocky and uncertain.

The horse clawed and scrambled, fighting desperately for footing. His lurching threw Joe back and forth in his saddle.

Inwardly he smiled, aware that his lurching body presented a difficult target. Indeed, he had taken the roughest way deliberately, for this reason.

Under the pretense of searching the ascending glide for the best route, his eyes roved ceaselessly ahead, seeming to fix themselves on the trail but in reality scanning the slope all the way to its top. His glance located each possible bit of cover, and his mind catalogued them all, until they were behind and therefore of no further use.

Imperceptibly his muscles and nerves grew tight. His lips drew close against his teeth. His eyes narrowed further. A cold wind seemed to blow against him, though the day was warm.

Then his eyes caught it, the vaguest kind of movement behind a clump of thick brush halfway to the top.

His eyes caught it, but did not hold. Instead, they deliberately passed over the spot, made another sweep of the trail ahead, and negligently returned.

He knew instantly that he had overestimated Claude. That movement had not been shown him deliberately to test him. It had been shown him only because Claude could not help it.

Now Joe looked straight into the tiny, menacing bore of a rifle, into the slitted, squinted, deadly eyes behind it. Another instant and it would belch smoke and flame.

He was lost, but he had to try. His horse lurched, scrambling over a particularly rough portion of the slide, and Joe flung himself, aided by the horse's lunge, backward off the animal's rump.

He heard the rifle's bellow, and, hearing it, knew he had saved himself for the moment, at least. Then he hit the cruel, cutting rocks of the slide, and was rolling, being cut to ribbons by their razor-edged sharpness.

The rifle cracked again, spitefully, and the bullet shattered a rock not six inches from Joe's face. Its dust blinded him. Fragments stung his face and set it to bleeding in a dozen places, despite his heavy beard.

But his mind was at work, and the previously catalogued bits of cover now spread themselves before it. A bush at the right of the trail, a large rock at the left, a little farther back.

A corner of his eye caught the bush, too high to be reached without remaining exposed too long. The rock, then. He flung himself sideways, rolling, praying silently that his gun had not fallen from its holster during the fall and the subsequent roll down the steep slide.

A shower of small rocks, dislodged by his frightened horse, deluged him. Another rifle bullet probed for his body, and found the long muscles of his back, searing a gouge four inches long, but not penetrating.

Then his body was partly hidden by the rock, but his calves and feet were still exposed. A bullet struck between his feet, and he drew them up spasmodically.

A short lull, followed by another shot from Claude, a shot that narrowly missed smashing his right foot. He tried to draw it in still farther, and discovered he could not without exposing some other part of him.

An impossible situation. Given enough shots, Claude would smash his foot, and that could be almost as deadly as a more lethal shot, for it would disable him and make escape impossible.

He estimated the range at fifty yards, too far for precision shooting with a revolver. In any case, Joe's rifle was in the saddle boot, and his horse was now nearly to the top of the slide.

Suddenly all the waiting, all the torment, all the nerve-racking suspense of the past weeks built in his mind until inaction became no longer tolerable.

Joe stood up. His gun came from its holster, hammer cocked, with bewildering speed.

There was Claude, rifle level, eye squinted along the barrel. Joe's eyes bored into Claude's while his mind made allowance for wind and range, for shooting uphill.

The rifle cracked. But Claude had been frightened by Joe's foolhardy courage in standing up. The bullet buzzed harmlessly past Joe's head.

Claude tried to duck down, but Joe's bullet was on its way. It took Claude between the eyes and drove him back, to disappear from Joe's sight behind the bush.

With his back screaming its pain, with his body aching in every joint, Joe scrambled breathlessly upward, gun ready in his hand.

But there was no need. Claude lay lifeless where he had fallen.

Joe sat down, and for fifteen minutes trembled as though he had a chill. Sweat dripped from his face, trickling through his beard and dropping on his filthy shirt.

It came to him, quite suddenly, that all the ties were gone.

He got up and laid Claude out flat on the ground. Then, slowly and with some doubt, he unbuckled his own gun belt and laid it across Claude's body. After that, working slowly and steadily, he piled rocks upon body and gun until they were completely hidden under a layer two feet thick.

Joe felt naked as he struggled to the top of the slide, naked and defenseless without his gun. But the break had been made. Defenseless, he had no choice but to earn his keep the way other men did.

At the top of the slide, he dug a hole with the blade of his knife. He laid the gold-laden saddlebags in it and covered it over. Atop it he placed a single large, distinctively shaped rock.

Then he mounted his horse and rode up, entering a new country and a new life, or, if fate so decreed, death at the hands of the first man who recognized him.

CHAPTER SEVENTEEN

At dawn the next day, he rode into a long, shallow valley through which a narrow, twisting stream wandered.

Willows and cottonwoods, their leaves bright with autumn, lined the banks of the stream. Nestled in a grove of them, looking almost as though it had grown there, stood a tiny, one-room log cabin. Joe rode toward the cabin.

He was tired, both with the weariness of travel and with the exhaustion of emotions worn to the breaking point. He felt that if he had to spend another day with his own thoughts, he'd go mad.

But there were no towns in this part of Wyoming. The cabin would have to do.

A plume of blue-gray smoke spiraled from the cabin's stone chimney. Joe swung down before the door and hailed, "Hey! Anybody home?"

"Yeah. I'm home." The voice came from behind him.

Joe swung nervously. His right hand made a useless motion. Then he grinned helplessly.

The man he faced was three times his age or more. His

face was covered with a three-day growth of graying whiskers. His eyes were blue, penetrating, his skin as seamed and brown as the stock of the rifle he held in his hands.

The man's expression was one of withheld judgment, neither approving nor entirely disapproving. He said, with some surprise, "Hell, you ain't no more'n a kid. But it looks like somebody's been usin' you damned hard." The stranger seemed to be studying Joe's eyes, as though the answer he sought lay there.

Joe didn't quite know what to say. He was used to many things, but not to this probing curiousness.

The man's eyes ranged over him, from his ragged shirt, caked with blood on its back, to his face, bearded and scarred with stone fragments, his bloodshot, weary eyes. They touched his pants, and did not miss the shiny, worn place where the holster had rubbed. The man's eyes said he was hesitating between two verdicts.

He came to no apparent decision. But he shifted the rifle to his left hand and stuck out his right. His face creased into a smile that had its reservations. But it was at least a smile.

The man said, "Robineau. Dell Robineau. This here's my outfit, and it sure as hell gets lonesome since . . ." His face clouded. Then, as quickly as the change had come, it was gone. He said, "Hell, what I mean is, I'm glad to see any man, even the kind that keeps lookin' over his shoulder all the time. Take your horse over there to the barn. That's what I call the shack out behind the cabin. They's oats in a bin, and a couple of forkfuls of hay likely wouldn't go amiss from the looks of that hoss you're ridin'. I'll just go in the house an' stir up some grub."

Joe stared at him a moment. No questions. Just a sharp pair of eyes that looked and missed nothing.

Bewildered, Joe led his horse to the shed, which was a one-stall barn with a partitioned tack room next to the stall. He put his horse into the stall and gave him a gallon can full of oats from the bin. Then he threw a couple of forkfuls of hay in the manger.

He offsaddled while the horse nuzzled the unfamiliar but fascinating grain. He rubbed the horse down with an old sack. Then he went out and closed the door.

From the cabin wafted the tantalizing smell of frying meat. Joe went to the door and looked in. Robineau stood at the stove, turning inch-thick antelope steaks in a cast-iron skillet.

By way of explanation, Joe started, "I . . ."

The man interrupted. "Never mind, kid. I ain't blind. You've been packin' a gun that you were likely mighty handy with. Maybe you killed somebody, maybe not. Point is, you ain't wearin' the gun now. You don't have to give me your life's story."

Joe was silent.

"You're tired of your own thoughts and figured if you didn't find somebody to talk to, you'd go nuts. Ain't that about it?"

Joe nodded helplessly, wondering whether to be angry or not.

Robineau turned back to the steaks. "Maybe I know how you feel. Maybe I felt thataway once myself."

Joe couldn't help asking, "What did you do?"

"I threw the gun away too. I came here an' built this cabin. After a while I found me a woman." He glanced around at Joe.

Joe's glance questioned him.

"She's dead. Been dead almost fifteen years. Ever since the boy was five."

"Then you've got a son?"

Bitterness came to the man's face and went away. "Had one. Now he's dead too. You can chalk that one up to the Wyoming Cattle Growers Association. We had a ruckus up here several years ago. Didn't have a name then. Just a ruckus. But now folks are beginnin' to call it the Johnson County War. My kid, now, he felt pretty strongly about things. Nothin' would do but he'd get in the middle of it."

Joe didn't know what to say, so he said nothing. After a short silence, Robineau went on: "Funny. Kids won't listen much. They got to find things out for themselves. They've got no patience and they can't wait. Things is either black or white to them. But when a man gets older—well, he learns. My kid would have been about your age, maybe a year or two older."

Robineau nodded toward the table. "Set a couple of plates out on the table. Grub's ready."

Joe did. Knives and forks and spoons, too, and tin cups for coffee.

There was meat enough to feed half a dozen men. And fried potatoes. And sour-dough biscuits from the oven. A feast after the way a man lived on the trail.

Joe ate ravenously. After supper Robineau said, "I'll put water on to heat. You'll want a bath." He looked at Joe closely. "Tell me one thing. You done anything that'd make a man ashamed of havin' hid you out?"

This was personal, and Joe felt a stir of resentment.

Robineau's steady regard disturbed him. But suddenly Joe grinned. "It'd depend on the man, I guess."

"Me?"

"I don't think you would. I haven't shot anybody in the back, if that's what you mean."

He had the odd feeling that Robineau had not heard his words. Robineau had been studying his face. The man nodded. "All right. My razor's over there on the shelf. Shave, but leave yourself a mustache. Makes a man look different if he's never worn one before. Older. I'll dig out some of my kid's clothes. Anybody on your trail—close?"

Joe shook his head, wondering how much he should tell. Finally he said, "No pictures out on me, either. Descriptions is all."

Robineau said doubtfully, "You can stay a while, I guess. Till the heat's off. No wages, though. Grub an' smokin' money is all. Move on any time you take the notion. If you stay here, you're my brother's boy from Kansas."

Joe tried to stammer his thanks, but Robineau cut him short with a wave of his hand, seemingly reassured by what he saw in Joe's face. "Forget it. I ain't so old but what I can remember the way I felt when I was in your fix. I figured the whole human race was nothin' but a bunch of bastards. Only they ain't." He grinned unexpectedly. "They just act like it sometimes."

He lifted a copper wash boiler onto the stove. He poured in what was left of a bucket of water and then handed Joe the bucket. "Fill it in the stream. A decent bath will take about five buckets."

Joe went out. For some reason, he was thinking about Ed Mallory. Maybe it was because Dell Robineau reminded him of Ed.

— —

The days passed. To Joe, it was good to work again. It was good to feel the surging power of a running cow horse under him, to feel a lariat running through his hands. It was good to feel the handles of a post-hole digger, good when the sweat darkened his shirt and dripped from his brow. If a man worked, he could sometimes forget a while all that had gone before.

Neither Joe nor Dell worked by the clock. They didn't even have one. They rose half an hour before dawn, and they rode and worked till dark. Then they stopped.

Slowly, as the days merged into weeks, the reservation went out of Dell Robineau's eyes. Gradually he began to look at Joe with approval, with liking, and sometimes even with affection.

Winter came, bringing its leaden skies, its icy winds, its driving blizzards. For days they would huddle inside the snug cabin, playing two-handed poker for matches with a deck of dog-eared cards. Then the sun would break through, making the rolling plain a thing of almost dazzling beauty, and they'd go to work again.

A couple of drifters came through, heading for Arizona, and Joe wrote Molly a letter after they'd promised to mail it from Tucson.

Joe had a time with the letter. For one thing, he'd never written one before. For another, he didn't quite know what to say. He'd promised to send for Molly and he hadn't done it. There were reasons why he hadn't, but Molly didn't know them.

At last he wrote, "Dear Molly: I expect you've heard

things about me you don't like. Maybe you've even got tired of waiting and married somebody else. I wouldn't blame you if you had. But someday I'm coming back. If you're still there when I do, I'll make you marry me. I haven't changed the way I feel about you. I'll never change." He signed it, "Joe."

As he wrote, the memory of her came back so strong it almost choked him. He wanted to put so much more into the letter and he hadn't the words. But he hoped Molly would read his yearning between the stilted lines, would feel the love that had been in his heart as he penciled its awkward words.

Spring came, and green grass was like a glorious blanket across the land. Together he and Robineau rode, branding calves wherever they found them. Robineau had only a small herd, slightly more than a hundred cows. They tallied, and afterward rode thirty miles in all directions, hunting strays.

Now Joe began to meet Robineau's neighbors. There were the Beckworths, husband, wife, and two rowdy boys. There was Sim Hartman, hardly older than Joe, and his plain, smiling wife. There was Jess Browne, as old and gnarled as an ancient cedar, who lived alone. They welcomed Joe, and accepted him as Robineau's nephew without question.

The spring came, and summer, and the sharp, cool days of autumn. Joe Redenko was Joe Robineau now, accepted by everyone within a three-day ride of Robineau's cabin.

They drove their beef to Casper, and shipped to Omaha, and they had a night on the town during which Joe met the sheriff and shook his hand and was not recognized. He began, for the first time, to feel safe again.

Back to the cabin for the winter, but now there was a restlessness in Joe. And Dell Robineau understood it.

"Go get her, boy. Maybe she's still waitin'. How the hell you ever goin' to know if you don't go see? I'm gettin' too damned old to spend the winter out here, anyways. It'd be a heap nicer for an old duffer to have a room in town, where the saloon's nearby an' the talk's plentiful. Thataway, you c'd have this place all to yourselves for the winter."

Joe looked at him, something burning behind his eyes, his throat closing so that he could hardly speak. There was a difference in Robineau since the time Joe had first seen him. The man looked older, and his skin had not the same healthy, leathery color, but more of a gray tone to it. His eyes, at first so blue and sharp, were fading.

Going, too, was his ambition, his get-up-and-go. Often now he wouldn't rise until breakfast was on the table. He worked less, leaving more and more of the chores to Joe. Mostly Robineau just liked to sit on the tiny porch and let the sun pour down upon him.

Joe said, "No. Not until spring. Not until after the calf-branding's done. Then I'll go. But hell, likely she's married by now. Likely she's plumb forgot me." There were a couple of reasons why Joe put it off. One was money. He hadn't any, and he couldn't go to Molly without anything. Nor could he ask Robineau for any. That hadn't been their deal.

Robineau shook his head. "She ain't forgot you if she's like you said she was."

But Joe wasn't so sure. He'd wavered himself when there had seemed no hope. Why, then, should not Molly waver when she had never known real hope since the day Joe left?

Robineau cleared his throat. "I . . . I filled out a paper an' left it in town when we shipped. It says this here place an' the cattle an' horses go to you if somethin' should happen to me."

Joe's throat was tight again. "Why? Why the hell should you do that for me?" His voice sounded angry.

Robineau laughed embarrassedly. "Why the hell not? Who else would I give it to? I sure can't take it with me. And anyhow, I figure you've earned a big slice of it. You've worked around here more'n a year for nothin' but your keep. Besides, you remember what I told you the day you came? I was in your fix once. Only the country was different then. There wasn't lawmen around everywhere you looked. I could make my own way, just by settlin' an' buildin' a cabin. You can't. Things is different from what they used to be."

Joe protested, "But I don't need it. I got money. I got a whole sackful of money." And he had, too. Only it was money he would never touch.

Dell grunted. "Buried somewhere? You don't want the damn stuff. Send Ed Mallory a letter. Tell him where it is. Let him return it to them as owns it by right."

Joe muttered angrily, "Later, maybe. Right now I don't know what the hell all this jawing is about. You'll live to be a hundred."

"Sure. Sure I will."

"Anyway, Dell, I . . . Oh, Christ!" It was all Joe could say. He'd never learned to say thanks properly. He remembered suddenly, for no particular reason, the surly way he'd sent Molly Ledbetter away that day behind the school when she'd offered to eat lunch with him. He realized that he'd never once thanked Ed Mallory for taking him in, for all Ed had done for him.

He'd been so busy hating the people who hurt him and resenting the hurts that he hadn't given much thought to anything else.

So the blame lay, and Joe knew it now, not entirely on the people of Du Bois. Part of it lay on Joe himself.

Robineau said, "Get out the cards. I feel like a game."

Joe got them down, and they began to play.

It was a winter of storm, a terrible winter by any standards. For days on end the blizzard wind howled about the cabin's eaves and rattled its windows. Snow sifted in through the tiny window and door cracks and made drifts on the floor.

When it would clear for a while, Dell and Joe would ride, trying to check their cattle's drift, trying to drive those that had found no shelter to where it might be found. They had losses, but the losses were not so great as they might have been. Robineau's cattle were natives and hardy, used to the icy winds of winter.

The days passed, and Joe thought of spring. True, he still had no money, and no prospects of getting any. But he had a way of life to offer Molly, or would have in the spring, when he would be able, with a clear conscience, to leave Robineau for a while.

Suppose there were no money? It didn't matter. Joe could manage to provide their needs.

So he dreamed of spring, and of Molly. He would ride into Du Bois in the night to tap softly on Molly's window.

She would come to him, clad only in her sheer nightgown, and would cling to him in a way that would make his blood run hot as molten iron. Then he'd carry her away, wrapped in a blanket, held across his saddle before him so that he could look at her.

She would not be changed. In Joe's mind, steadfast Molly could never change. She would see at last that Ledbetter had already done all to Joe that he could do. She would consent to marry Joe, free from fear at last.

And yet there were times when uneasiness crept into Joe's dreams. This, perhaps, was cold reasoning, logic, which has no place in dreams.

Cold logic told Joe he was being a fool. Molly had not waited. Molly was already married.

There was no use in going back. The dreams were all Joe had, and he would not go back, lest he lose even his dreams.

CHAPTER EIGHTEEN

Spring came, as it always does, but its coming seemed unnaturally slow to Joe, for all his decision not to return for Molly.

As always in the high plains, spring was as unpredictable as a woman, of varying moods from warm, budding gentleness to chilling rain or raging sleet.

They were out riding, branding, when the storm struck them. They were fifteen miles from the cabin.

All morning it had been warm, perhaps unseasonably so. But at noon the sky began to cloud up, the wind to chill.

Joe was frying steaks over a tiny fire when the first grain

of sleet struck his face. He looked at Dell. "We ought to be getting back. All either of us has got is a thin jumper."

"No hurry. We'll have the wind at our backs."

So they finished eating before they rode. And by that time the air was choked with pelting, frozen balls of sleet. The wind came up, nearing hurricane velocity. In half an hour their backs were soaked.

They began to hurry over the ground that was turning to a slippery sea of mud. Days of hot sun had warmed it, and now the sleet melted almost as fast as it fell.

Suddenly Dell's horse went to his knees. He fought for footing, but there was none. He slid to the edge of a wash, and plummeted into it.

Dell stayed with him, fighting. The horse rolled in a welter of flailing hoofs, and Dell was pinned beneath the saddle. A single pain-filled shout escaped his lips.

Joe swung off his horse. By the time he got to the bottom of the wash, the horse was up covered with mud, shaking himself and trembling with fright. Joe spoke soothingly.

Dell was getting up, too, favoring one leg. Joe breathed a sigh of relief. Dell was shaken, perhaps bruised, but he wasn't injured.

And then Joe stopped, the grin that had grown on his face rapidly evaporating. For Dell had fallen into six inches of watery mud. He was soaked to the skin.

Dell looked at him sheepishly. "Looks like the damn fool could have picked a better place to fall. If you laugh, goddamn you, I'll bust you one."

Joe said, "I'm not laughing. We need a fire—fast."

"And what the hell would you build a fire with?"

"But you're wet." He began to peel off his jacket.

"Change with me."

"Are you crazy? Get on your goddamn horse. We'll be home in another thirty minutes."

Dell gave him no chance to argue. He caught his horse and mounted, and while Joe was still putting his jacket back on, he spurred the horse away.

Joe mounted his own horse and followed. He caught Dell half a mile farther on, and Dell was blue with cold, his teeth chattering audibly. Joe said, "If you won't change clothes, at least get down and walk. Work up some circulation. Warm yourself up."

"Hell with you. What I need is a stove and a slug of whisky."

They made it to the house, where Dell stripped and went to bed. Joe built up the fire until the cabin was steaming hot. He spiked a cup of coffee heavily with whisky and gave it to the older man. Dell drank it, lay back, and went to sleep.

Joe changed his own clothes and prepared some supper, which Dell ate with good appetite. When darkness came, Joe crawled into the other bunk and went to sleep himself.

In the morning, there were no signs of the sleet storm left outside save for the wetness of the ground, steaming now in a hot sun.

But inside the cabin there were more serious consequences. For Dell had a raging fever.

All day it grew worse. Joe gave him quinine and whisky, but it seemed to help not at all. The next day Dell was out of his head, and began to cough. And that afternoon another sleet storm struck.

Joe was ready to go, ready for the seventy-mile ride to

Casper for a doctor. The sleet storm stopped him. He was afraid to leave Dell alone, afraid Dell could not keep up the fire, afraid even that Dell might wander out into the storm.

Seventy miles. Even if he killed a horse going and another coming back, Dell would be alone nearly twenty-four hours. No. The best course was to stay with Dell, to stay and do what he could.

Perhaps the fever would pass. Perhaps if Joe kept him eating and warm, the fever would pass.

But it didn't. And late that night, Dell woke Joe by calling to him. Joe lighted the lamp and sat down beside the old man's bed. Dell croaked, "I feel like hell—worse'n I ever have before. You reckon I might not make it, Joe?"

"You'll make it, you old he-alligator."

"Maybe. But if I don't, I want you to promise me some-thin'.

"Go after that girl—Molly. Slip into town and out again without nobody knowin' you're there, if you want. But go back for her. Give her a chance to say no if she wants to."

Joe looked at him. It was in his mind to refuse, but after a look at Dell's eyes, he couldn't. He nodded. "I promise."

Dell grinned at him. "I'd like to hear a woman's laugh in this house again. I'd like to hear a baby cry."

Joe said, "Maybe you will." But he knew Dell wouldn't. Dell had been weakening for more than a year. He had not enough strength left to fight this raging fever, this whooping, rasping cough that left him sweating and weak and gasping for breath.

Joe sat up beside Dell for the rest of the night, watching the irregular rise and fall of his chest. Helpless and tortured, he saw that bellows slow and finally stop altogether. And for the first time in many a month, Joe buried his face in the blankets and wept.

It was noon before he could bring himself to leave. He rode out, galloping, and went to the Beckworths'. Afterward he came home and waited for them to arrive.

The Beckworths came in a buckboard, with a new pine casket in the back. Sim Hartman brought his wife in a buggy, loaded down with cooked food dishes and fresh baked pies. Jess Browne came on horseback, carrying an old black Bible that must have weighed ten pounds.

Jess dressed Dell in his best and shaved him. Then he laid him in the casket, which was lined with black silk. Sim Hartman and Joe, working in shifts, dug the grave in the muddy ground.

Jess, who in his younger years had been a lay minister, preached a short service. When night came, they were gone, and Joe was alone.

In the succeeding days he buried himself in work. He finished branding, and tallied, and rode to gather strays. He traveled to Casper, to settle Dell's affairs, and made a report to the coroner on the cause of death. And he bought a secondhand gun, because he was going to go back for Molly now, and a sensible man does not enter enemy territory with no means of defending himself. He would rather die himself than use the gun to kill anyone, but sometimes the mere presence of a gun close to a steady hand is enough to save a man serious trouble.

And so it was mid-June before he was ready to ride toward Du Bois, and early July before he reached a point on the plateau from which he could look down on the town.

He could see no difference. There was the stone bank

building, dingy and squat in the bright sunlight. There was the jail, the hotel, the monstrous livery barn. Joe picked out the school, Molly's tree-shaded house, Ed's house, Rafferty's saloon.

His eyes followed the road that led southwest into the Du Bois canyon, the route he had taken when leaving some four years before. They picked out the islands significant in Joe's life. They had changed shape in the four years Joe had been gone, but otherwise were just the same.

It seemed impossible to Joe that the years, which had dealt so harshly with him, should have touched the town so lightly. And it occurred to him that if he should walk into Ledbetter's bank he would find it precisely the same, with Susan Poole sitting on her high stool at the barred window taking deposits with her dry courtesy, with Roscoe Ledbetter at a desk in the back, granting and refusing loans with the same cold, businesslike precision.

Ed Mallory would be in the sheriff's office, his feet on the desk. And Sam Breen would be down in the store.

Willie would be different, and probably Molly too. If they were married to each other . . . Joe's face twisted. God, don't let them be married. Don't let her be different. Please.

He sat on the rim and watched the antlike figures of the people in town until sundown. Then he mounted and found the trail that led down through the rimrock toward the valley below.

So far, he had met not a soul ascending the plateau, sixty miles north, but this was not entirely chance. He had kept his eyes peeled and had avoided contact with the few other humans he saw. He continued to do so now. Entering town, he twice reined back into the shelter of a bunch of trees to wait until someone had passed.

A dog discovered him, and barked. Another took up the cry, and before long there were four of them yapping at his horse's heels. Someone came to the door of a house nearby and called querulously, "Who is it? Who's there?"

Joe didn't answer and the door closed. He cursed the dogs bitterly, and they quieted and slunk away, losing interest immediately in this man who seemed to know all the right words.

Joe took the shortest route to Ed's house that would afford him a maximum of cover. And since it was the supper hour, when everyone was indoors eating, he made it without being seen.

He might have walked out of Ed's stable only yesterday, for all the change he could detect. Even the smell was the same. The grain was in the same place, and atop it even the same old gallon berry can they had used to measure it. The hay fork that Joe had used so many times he found in its accustomed place, and he threw down three forkfuls for his horse. But he did not unsaddle. He only loosened the cinch.

He went up the creaking boardwalk from stable to back door, and knocked lightly.

Ed's voice came from the kitchen. "Come on in."

Joe entered and crossed the back porch. He opened the kitchen door and stepped in swiftly, bringing it closed behind him with a single movement. Ed looked up.

He was older. A lot older. The years had dealt no less harshly with Ed than they had with Joe. He was thinner, too.

At first Joe saw only pure amazement in his face. Then there was gladness, gladness that grew into a wide, happy grin.

Ed shoved his chair back and crossed the room. He put his arms around Joe and hugged him as though he were a child. When he drew away, his eyes were bright with moisture, which he blinked away shamefacedly. "Joe! Goddamnit, I ain't never been so glad to see anyone! Sit down and have some supper."

Joe sat down and ate with famished concentration. He ate quickly, the question he had to ask Ed burning in his thoughts. When he had finished he looked up fearfully at Ed. His voice was hoarse, hardly more than a whisper. "How about Molly, Ed? Is she married?"

He waited with held breath for Ed's answer, which was a slowly shaking head. Joe's blood raced. Then he saw in Ed's eyes a look that had been there before. It was a look of withdrawn approval, of outright reserve.

Joe said quickly, "I've got to have her, Ed. I'll make her go with me."

Ed's expression was unchanging. He said, "You and her and the Allens, huh?"

Joe shook his head. "The Allens are dead, both of them. The money is buried in Wyoming, just north of the Colorado line."

Quickly he described the place to Ed so that Ed could find it. "I don't want it. I want to know if you'll go get it and see that it gets back to the people that it belongs to."

Ed nodded. Part of his reserve melted, but only a part.

Joe said desperately, "I want you to go tell Molly I'm here. Bring her back with you."

Ed's voice was cold. "You figure that what you've got to offer is good enough—a life of running, of hiding out, of never knowing when a hand will tap your shoulder and you'll have to kill again?"

Joe shook his head defensively. "I know it isn't good enough. But I can try to make it better, can't I?" He went on before Ed could speak. "Nobody'll be looking for me for killing the Allens. If you return the money there won't be much pressure on that account. It's only James Nordley."

Suddenly his voice was dead, without hope. He said, "I guess you're right, Ed. It isn't good enough. They'll hunt me forever for killing Nordley. But Ed, I tried. I swear I tried. When I saw the star on his shirt I tried to miss. It was just too late." He fished makings from his pocket, and made a smoke with fingers that trembled. His shoulders seemed to sag. "No, it just isn't good enough for Molly."

He looked at Ed and the reserve was fading from Ed's eyes. The old sheriff said, "Maybe you'd better let her decide. You see, Joe, Nordley didn't die. He's not the man he used to be, but he's still alive." He got up and reached for his coat. "You wait here. I'll bring Molly."

Joe was too stunned to move.

Ed said, "It was Nordley that bothered me. You understand that, Joe? I had to know how it was the day you shot him."

"Sure, Ed." Joe was grinning now himself. "Get out of here. Get Molly. Hurry."

Ed closed the door behind him. For a moment Joe sat utterly still. He felt as though a load had been lifted from his back.

He couldn't sit still. How would it be with Molly? Did she remember the warm nights on the island, the wonder, the magic of it? Or had the years embittered her? Had she found someone else? Would she be indifferent toward Joe?

He paced the floor like a caged wolf. And then at last he heard a sound. The sound of running feet.

For an instant all the cold wariness returned. Then it was gone. For the sounds were too light to be a man's footsteps.

The door burst open, and Molly was across the room with a flurry of excited, breathless movement.

No words, unless her gasp of pure joy could be called a word. Then her arms were tight around his neck, tight and clinging and demanding with the suppressed hunger and longing of four years.

Her body was warm, tight against him. Soft lips burned against his own. Tears wet her cheeks and rubbed off onto his own. Then she was weeping, as though the years had been too much, too many. Joe held her lightly now, tenderly, and whispered words that had no meaning, just sounds that were soothing and gentle.

Ed slammed the door and they drew apart. With his arm around her, Joe looked at Ed. Ed said, grinning, "Ask her, Joe. You know how it's done."

Joe held her at arm's length. "Will you marry me now, Molly?"

She smiled through her tears. She nodded. "Joe, I was such a fool!"

Joe felt his own eyes smarting. He said, "We'll have to slip away. You'll never be able to write, or see your mother and father again. Because if you did, your old man would track me down. It's a lot to ask, Molly."

She smiled. "I've had four years to think about it. I don't have to think any more."

She wasn't changed—at least, not much. Thinner, perhaps, but it only made her more beautiful. There was a maturity in her face that was new, which again only heightened her beauty.

A woman a man could cherish as a priceless treasure. A woman a man could die for, or live for, and exult in doing either.

Joe stopped talking and stared across the pitch-black, tiny cow-camp cabin at where he knew Ed was sitting. Right now it looked as if he was going to die for Molly.

Ed said hurriedly, "What about Willie Breen? What happened? Talk fast, Joe. We haven't got more than ten minutes left."

Joe wrung his sweaty hands together. He knew that death was close, and its hand was cold around his heart. But perhaps in talking he would be able to forget death for a moment. And so his words began again, tumbling out in disorderly confusion.

CHAPTER NINETEEN

They sat in the kitchen and talked for half an hour, Ed Mallory, Molly Ledbetter, and Joe Redenko. For Joe it had been like coming home.

Ed got up. "There's some things I ought to do down at the sheriff's office. I'll be back in an hour. You two settle things between yourselves. If you want to leave tonight, Joe, I'll give you horses. Ledbetter will swear out a warrant, of course, but I'll lead him off some other way and lose him. You'll have your chance."

They didn't answer. They sat together on a narrow, leather-covered sofa that seemed out of place in a kitchen. They were looking at each other and apparently did not even know he had left.

Molly came to his arms again, starved by the years' separation. Her kisses made his blood run fierce and fast.

Both heard the noise at the window. Both were aware of it for almost a minute without placing its source. At first it was a continuing sound, like that of a panting dog on a hot day, only more hoarse and rasping.

Uneasiness ran like a chill along Joe's spine. He pushed Molly away and stood up. He looked around the room, trying to place the sound, and as suddenly as it had begun, it stopped.

But from the window came a single sharp, crackling noise.

Joe ran to the door and plunged outside. He could see nothing. He walked over to the window. There was a lilac bush beside it, and Joe knew the bush had caused the crackling noise.

Someone had stood at the window, breathing harshly, watching them. When Joe stood up, whoever it was had fled. In turning, he had stepped into the bush, making it crackle.

Joe went back to the door. Molly stood framed in it. He said quickly, "Get back inside. Get out of the light."

"What is it, Joe?"

"Someone was watching us from outside the window. We'd better not wait for Ed. We'd better be on our way."

"There are some things I'd like to take. Just a very few. Could we take enough time for me to get them?"

Joe hesitated. It was dangerous. Someone knew he was in town. And Molly might be questioned if she went home and left again right away with her things. But how could a man ask his bride to come to him with nothing but the clothes on her back, particularly when he had nothing to offer her himself?

He said, "We'll take the time. It'll be all right."

Her smile of relief and gratitude was all the thanks he needed. He said, "But hurry. Make it fast. And don't let anyone see you."

"All right, Joe."

Joe blew out the lamp in Ed's kitchen. He drew her to him, kissed her, and then pushed her out the door.

He went back and sat down, without lighting the lamp. Who had it been at the window? And having seen Joe Redenko, a known outlaw, what would the person do?

Ed came back about fifteen minutes later. He came into the darkened kitchen and struck a match. Joe said, "Don't light the lamp, Ed."

"What's the matter? Where's Molly?"

"She went after some things." He paused. "Ed, somebody knows I'm in town. Somebody was looking in the window at Molly and me a while ago."

Ed whistled. "Know who it was?"

"No idea." But his mind was beginning to add things up. No one had seen him come here. He was sure of that. Therefore, it must have been someone who had followed Molly and Ed.

But who would be following Molly? Her father? Willie Breen? Some other young man who was interested in her?

Joe asked, "Who's been after Molly since I've been

gone, Ed?"

"Couple of cowboys, usually. By the time one gets discouraged, there's another to take his place."

"Who else?"

"Willie. Who do you think? He hasn't been makin' any headway, though. Molly won't have anything to do with him. But I've seen him hangin' around in front of her house a time or two. Just standin' there, watchin' the house the way a hungry cat watches the barn at milkin' time."

"Then that's who it must have been. He saw you come after Molly. He figured that was funny, so he followed the two of you."

Ed whistled again, this time worriedly. "Joe, you know what Willie will do, don't you? He'll run straight to his old man, and then to Ledbetter. Come on. Let's get the hell out of here. We'll take your horse and one of mine and catch Molly on her way back here."

Joe got up. He crossed the kitchen and yanked open the back door. He heard the yell, around front, immediately. "Ed! Damn you, we know Joe's in there. And Molly too. Send her out, Ed, or there's going to be more trouble than you and he both can handle."

Neither Joe nor Ed answered. They stood there by the open door silently, scarcely breathing.

The voice came again, Ledbetter's angry bellow: "Goddamn you, Ed, answer me! I'll see you get run out of the country for this, after we get through with that damned hunky!"

Joe could hear Ed's low chuckle. "Riled, ain't he?"

Joe said bitterly, "Now what? What the hell do I do now?"

"Take it easy. We'll work this out if I have to jail the three of them till you get away. You stay here. I'll go to the front door and talk to them. While we're talking, you slip out back. Get the horses and hightail it over to Molly's after her. I'll keep them jawing here till you get clear."

Joe hesitated. "It'll cost you your job, Ed."

He could sense Ed's old, reckless grin even though he couldn't see it. "What if it does? It'll be worth it. It'll be worth the job to see Ledbetter's face when I tell him you an' Molly are gone."

Joe's hand gripped the Sheriff's shoulder. Then Ed was gone.

Joe waited until he heard the Sheriff's shout from the front door. Ed yelled, "Now. What the hell's all this about?"

Ledbetter shouted back, "Quit the stalling, Ed. Willie saw him. He saw Molly with Joe inside your house."

"What was Willie doing, Roscoe? Has Willie taken to sneaking around at night peeking into other people's windows?"

Joe's mouth twisted a little at that, yet it wasn't really a grin. Because there wasn't anything funny about either Willie or the situation he had created. Joe had been so close, so damned close, to getting clear with Molly. And Willie had ruined it.

As he stepped out the, door, Joe felt a sudden attack of uneasiness. It was almost as though he expected . . .

He stopped abruptly, for he knew what it was. He hadn't heard Willie's voice out there in front. He hadn't heard Ledbetter or Breen speak to him, either.

Then Willie could be here. He could be lurking here in the yard watching the back door. And if he were here, he'd be angry and jealous enough to be dangerous.

Joe's body seemed to crouch. He tensed for the dash across the yard to the stable.

His eyes caught the flash, and an instant later the roar of a revolver smashed against his eardrums.

Joe dropped, his gun already in his hand. He was untouched, but he could feel fury stirring in his brain. He rolled, and raised his revolver, but then he let it drop again. Shoot Willie? He could do nothing that would more quickly doom his and Molly's plans.

No, he'd wait it out for a few moments. Maybe something would happen. Maybe Willie would get scared and run away. Or maybe Ed would come rushing out back and in the confusion give Joe a chance to get away.

Joe began to crawl, inching his way toward the stable. His hand touched a rusty piece of chain, and it rattled faintly.

Again Willie's gun roared as he fired at the sound. The bullet kicked up a shower of dirt a foot from Joe's head.

Carefully Joe began to crawl again. It was almost completely dark here in the yard, save for the small amount of light from the stars.

He was now almost halfway across the yard. Another few feet and he'd risk getting up, making a dash for the stable. He wouldn't have time to saddle one of Ed's horses. He'd have to make his own do, and later buy a horse for Molly at some outlying ranch.

He inched forward. He was now but a short fifteen feet from the stable. He rose to a crouch, preparatory to leaping to his feet.

He didn't know whether Willie heard the slight noise he

made, or whether Willie saw him. But Willie's revolver blasted for a third time, and the bullet burned like a hot iron across the flat muscles of Joe's back.

For the briefest instant the pain was maddening. In pain and not immediately realizing that he had only been creased, Joe reacted instinctively.

He came to his feet, whirling smoothly and without waste motion. It was almost as it had been so long ago, the day he faced Nordley. He was not thinking, but reacting with pure instinct.

The hammer was back on his revolver, and he squeezed off a single shot in the direction of Willie's muzzle flash.

Normally, Joe would have squeezed off several shots before he stopped. Tonight, however, something stopped him. It may have been that reason immediately overpowered the instinct that had made him shoot. Or it may have been a sound he heard, so slight and so close on the heels of his shot that a man might almost think he had imagined it.

Except that the sound was familiar. It was the sound of a bullet striking living human flesh.

Immediately Joe's gun slid back into its holster. He began to run, but this time he did not run toward the stable, but toward the place where Willie's gun had flashed.

There was danger in doing so, of that he was well aware. But suddenly he cared no longer for danger. He only knew he had to ease the sinking feeling inside his stomach. He had to know if he had killed again.

His foot struck something yielding, and he fell headlong. As he struggled to his feet, he could hear the crashing sounds made by Ledbetter and Breen as they came running around Ed's house through the high weeds.

Inside the house, light flared as Ed lighted a lantern, and then Ed came running out the door, carrying it.

For a split second its wavering light fell upon Willie's inert body. Joe saw the bullet hole, and it was squarely in the middle of Willie's back.

Ed's eyes must have been blinded momentarily by the lantern. Possibly Ledbetter and Breen were blinded too, having looked across at Ed and his lantern as he came out the door.

Joe got up and ran. He ran around behind the stable, to enter by the big rear carriage doors.

Momentarily screened by the stable, and in darkness again, he halted briefly, shocked and horrified by what he had done, but puzzled too.

Why had the bullet struck Willie in the back? And why had he been lying on his stomach, with his head farthest from Joe?

Instantly Joe knew the answer. Willie had panicked after his last shot. Maybe he'd seen Joe rise and turn toward him. And Willie had turned to run. As he did, Joe's bullet had caught him.

But who in the town of Du Bois would believe that? Would Breen believe it? Would Ledbetter, crazed already with hatred?

Joe knew they wouldn't. Nor would any of the rest of the town believe, save perhaps for Ed Mallory.

And what could Ed do in the face of a town that howled for Joe's blood?

No. Willie had won, even in death. He had made Joe run again. He had spoiled what chance Joe had of taking Molly with him. He had perhaps even spoiled Joe's chance for life.

Joe opened the stable doors quietly. He tightened the cinch on his saddle and led the horse outside.

Ledbetter's bellow told him they'd found Willie. Joe vaulted into his saddle and spurred down the alley and out of town.

CHAPTER TWENTY

The inside of the old cow-camp cabin was now pitch black. Joe said, "That's how it happened, Ed. That's all of it. I rode upcountry until I hit the old Weatherbee trail. Then I came out on top. I'd have got away, too, if it hadn't been for my horse. He just gave out."

Ed said slowly, "I figured he would. I knew they'd get you as soon as I saw you hadn't taken one of mine. So I had no choice but to come along. They'd have got you, with or without me."

"Yeah. I know they would. I only wish I knew how Molly was taking this."

"How would you expect her to take it? She'd loved you since you were a kid and she was all set to go away with you. She's probably blaming herself for letting Willie follow her and me that night. But hell, that wasn't her fault. People don't expect other people to be following them around. Nobody does."

Joe heard a crashing of brush on the hillside behind the cabin. He said, "Looks like this is it, Ed. They're coming."

Joe was wondering how he'd take it. Would his courage hold when they put the noose around his neck? Would he be able to look them in the eye and die well, like a man?

He didn't know. He hoped he would. He didn't want to

give them this last satisfaction, that of seeing him go to pieces.

He said, "I guess I've been thinking mostly about myself. But this is tough for you, too. What are you going to do? You can't shoot it out with them—that'd be stupid." The bitterness was gone from his voice now, as though the talking had removed its cause.

But a certain coldness was creeping into Joe's body. Numbness crept over his mind. His hand, he realized, was gripping the handle of his revolver so hard that lack of blood circulation had stolen the hand's feeling and strength.

In the brush behind the cabin, Joe could hear voices, indistinguishable as to words, but unmistakable as to intent. He could hear the sounds of branches cracking as the lynchers broke the limbs from dead trees and piled them against the back wall of the cabin.

Joe knew what he ought to do. He ought to go out there and empty his gun into their ranks. He'd get two or three, even in the darkness, before they got him.

Sure. Why not? But he knew why not. His own plight would not be helped by killing innocent men, by making widows of women who had done nothing at all to deserve it.

How, then, would he go out? With his hands in the air so that they could have the pleasure of hanging him? Or fighting, shooting?

He knew, suddenly, how he'd go out. He'd go out with his hands in the air, with his gun left behind him in the cabin. He'd go as an innocent man should go, and then if they hanged him, the guilt of it would be theirs to live with, secretly and privately, all the rest of their lives.

Joe stepped to the door and pulled it wide. He unbuckled his gun belt and let it slip to the floor. There were other kinds of fighting than those he had learned so far. There was this kind, when the odds were mountainous against you, when you couldn't win and knew it.

The night was black and the stars gave little light. The air, moving into the open door, was cool, sharp with the chill of the altitude and the hour. Joe wondered briefly what Molly was doing now. He imagined her bitterly and helplessly weeping.

Joe heard Ledbetter's voice behind the cabin. "All right. A few more big branches. Then we'll light the dry grass we piled underneath and get back and surround the cabin. Remember, all of you, don't let the light from the fire catch you out in the open. We don't want any more dead men."

No. Take no chances. Shoot your prey down like a mad dog, from cover where he cannot see you and so fire back. Only tonight you were going to be fooled. You were going to have to hang the fugitive, so that afterward there would be no making excuses for yourselves.

Joe had, in his preoccupation, almost forgotten Ed. Now Ed stepped forward and touched his arm. "Pick up your gun and belt. We ain't finished yet."

Joe laughed, bitterly, almost soundlessly. "Stop it, Ed. This is it and you know it is."

"Uh-uh." Joe felt the smooth coldness of his gun as Ed thrust it into his hand. "I've been thinkin'. Those guys are watching for us to break out into the open. But half a dozen or so of them are busy as hell back behind the cabin getting their fire ready. If we jumped them now, they'd be so damned surprised they wouldn't know what to do."

"Jump them? Are you crazy? What good would it do to kill half a dozen of them? The rest would finish us off."

"Nobody said anything about killing."

"Then what do you mean?"

"I said jump them. We know Ledbetter's back there. We heard his voice. I'll lay you ten to one both Breen and Dalhart are there too."

"So?"

"The chance is slim, I'll admit. But if we could grab one of the three, or two of them, and get back inside this cabin, we'd have something to bargain with."

For a moment Joe was silent. It was a plan born of desperation, and he knew it. He knew Ed figured that way too. But hell, they *were* desperate, and it *was* a plan.

He shrugged. "It's all right with me. What have I got to lose?"

"Come on, then. You go around the right side of the cabin. I'll go around the left. Stick close to the wall and don't make a damned sound. When you get around in back, try to pick yourself a man. Likely it won't matter who you get. But I'd rather have either Ledbetter or Dalhart or Breen, because they're the leaders."

An odd tension was building up in Joe, but it was not an unpleasant thing. Rather it was exuberance, exhilaration. At least he was going to have a chance to do something. At least he didn't have to die helplessly.

Ed stepped out the door, and instantly blended into the darkness to become invisible. Joe followed. He looked into the darkness, searching for Ed, but Ed was gone.

Joe edged along, his back to the cabin wall, his feet

reaching, feeling for each step so that he would make no noise.

He turned the corner and stopped. He could see only the blackness of the nearby timber. But he could hear movement, and the almost continuous crackling of branches as they were dragged down and thrown upon the pile.

To hell with the noise. With all that the rest of them were making, they sure wouldn't hear what little Joe made.

Still sticking close to the wall, he moved down the length of the cabin. He tripped on a branch that protruded from the pile and almost fell.

Suddenly he grinned. The bunch of them was milling around here in the darkness like a flock of sheep. They thought Joe and Ed were safely inside the cabin. Dark as it was, Joe was willing to bet they wouldn't know him from one of their own if he moved out among them.

Then why not walk up the hill to safety, mingling with them until he had got clear?

He shook his head. They were stupid, maybe, but not that stupid. They'd have a ring of guards out there somewhere to guard against that very possibility.

No. Ed's idea had been the best. Joe grabbed a branch, lifted it off the pile, moved around behind the cabin, and flung it back onto the pile.

His stomach felt as though it were tied into a knot. He turned and headed up the hill.

He heard Ledbetter's exhortation to the men to hurry, off to his right, where Ed would be. And he bumped into a man, coming downhill carrying a large branch.

The man snarled, "Christ, why don't you stay out of the way?"

Joe didn't reply, for he knew this wasn't Breen, though the voice was oddly familiar. The man flung his burden onto the pile and turned to follow Joe.

And then suddenly Breen was coming downhill toward Joe, recognizable because of his short stature, his bulky body. It must be Breen, thought Joe. It's just got to be Breen.

Off to his right he heard a scuffle, and Ledbetter's startled yell, "It's Ed. Hey, look out! Ed's—"

There was a sodden thud and then a ponderous crash. Slugged him, thought Joe.

He lunged at Breen, but the man dropped the branch he was carrying and Joe plunged into it. His feet caught and he fell headlong, hopelessly tangled for a moment in the clawing limbs of the branch.

Before he could get clear, the man behind him piled on top of him. And Breen, thinking God knows what, began to fire into the tangle of struggling bodies.

Joe flung the man aside, getting up. He stumbled, still not clear of the tangling branch, and fell again, but this time he fell downhill. Breen's bullets were cutting viciously through the space where he had been but a moment before.

Now they were all coming, firing aimlessly, and Joe heard Breen's wild shout, "Hey! For crysake, hold it. I'm down here!"

Joe got up and started toward the sound of Breen's voice, filled with desperation now. Ed had done his part. Likely he had the inert body of Ledbetter in the cabin already. But Joe had fumbled his part. And now he had to redeem himself.

He lunged up the hill, trying to remember where that damned branch was that Breen had dropped. He collided violently with the body of a man, probably the one who had crashed into him before, and they struggled briefly. The man yelled, "Hey! I got him! I got him!"

Joe raised his gun to clout the man on the head, but his blow never descended. For a fusillade of shots broke out above, and Joe could feel the impact of several bullets thudding into the man he held. The man's body went limp and Joe dropped him.

Again he lunged up the hill, and this time it was Breen with whom he collided. Breen was down on his hands and knees, desperately trying to crawl away.

Joe's gun came down with a crack on Breen's skull. Then he gave Breen a flipping heave, and Breen rolled toward the bottom of the hill, with Joe lunging after him.

Once Joe fell across Breen's body. He was up in an instant intensely aware of the crashing sound of approaching feet. He rolled Breen again, and heard him come up with a crash against the wall of the cabin.

Then he was down there too, grasping Breen to drag him around the cabin to the door.

He felt a touch on his arm and whirled. His hand flashed toward the gun he had returned to its holster. Then he heard Ed's whisper, "Easy! I'll help you drag him in."

Ed grabbed one of Breen's arms, Joe the other. Bullets were now thudding steadily into the cabin wall. There was utter pandemonium above them on the hillside. Guns fired and men shouted frantically with fright and confusion.

They rounded the corner and heaved Breen inside.

Joe was panting furiously. Between breaths, he wheezed, "You get Ledbetter?"

"Uh-huh. Wait till I get my breath and I'll let the bastards know it. Who'd you get, Breen?"

"Yeah."

"All right. Watch the two of them, in case they come out of it."

Ed went to the door and yelled, "Hey out there!"

The shouting and the crashing back and forth through the timber slowed and finally stopped. Ed yelled, "I've got Breen and Ledbetter in here. Now simmer down, the whole goddamn bunch of you, and listen to what I've got to say!"

Joe heard a slight noise inside the cabin and toward the back wall in the silence that followed. An uneasy chill coursed along his spine. Had one or more of the lynchers sneaked inside while he and Ed were gone?

He snatched his gun from its holster and thumbed back the hammer. "Who's that? Sing out, damn it, or I'll shoot!"

He heard the sound again and nearly flung a shot toward it. In time he heard the voice, Molly's voice. "Joe, it's me."

"Oh, my God! How'd you get in here?"

"I slipped in while the commotion was going on out in back."

"Yeah, but how did you get here from town?"

Her voice was closer when she replied. He could smell her faint fragrance. "I got a horse and followed Ed and the men who were with him. I've been hiding out there in the timber all afternoon. Joe, if they'd caught you, I'm afraid I would have killed someone."

Joe put out his hand and touched her. He couldn't see her, but he could feel her hair, the way it was tangled and wind-whipped. He said, "You've got to get out of here."

"No, Joe. I'm going to stay. I belong here with you."

Ed's voice came from the door. "Quit the wrangling, you

two. Joe, you keep an eye on our unconscious friends."

"They're all right. They haven't stirred." He looked down at the blur that was Molly. He whispered, "It doesn't mean a hell of a lot, maybe, but we've got your old man and Breen. You keep quiet so none of the others will know you're here. Ed's figuring on your pa and Breen as hostages, but they won't be worth much if the mob knows you're in here too. They'd know we wouldn't hurt either Breen or your old man as long as you were in the cabin with us."

He wished Molly had stayed away. He doubted now, under the circumstances, whether either he or Ed could be very convincing about threatening Ledbetter and Breen.

But he had underestimated Ed. Ed yelled, "Like I said, I've got Ledbetter and Breen in here. You know what I'll do if you light that fire? I'll kill 'em both!"

A voice mocked, "The hell you will! You wouldn't like hangin' any better than the next man!"

"I wouldn't hang. And I'll tell you why. Every damned one of you is guilty right now of an attempt to commit murder. I'm a lawman. I can kill any one of you, stoppin' you, and still be in the clear so far as the law's concerned."

"But you won't."

"Won't I?" Something about Ed's tone sent a chill along Joe's spine.

Silence outside after that. Silence while the mob considered Ed's words and tone. Then a man shouted, "Why're you so damned set on savin' that killer? You know he's rotten, for all you raised him!"

"That's where you're wrong. Joe was leaving my place the other night. Willie cut down on him in the dark. Even so, Joe didn't shoot back right away. He didn't shoot back till Willie creased him. Trouble was, Willie'd lost his nerve and turned to run, only Joe didn't know it. He shot at Willie's last gun flash an' got Willie after Willie'd turned."

There was some discussion outside, which Ed interrupted. Ed was fighting now, no longer with gun and strength, but with words. The mob was slowed, but it wasn't stopped. Joe wondered where Dalhart was, and suddenly he placed the elusive familiarity he had noticed about the man he'd scuffled with behind the cabin. Dalhart. And Dalhart was either dead or badly wounded. He'd taken enough bullets in his body to kill a dozen men.

Ed yelled, "This is grudge business anyway. You're letting yourselves be used."

"Whaddaya mean, grudge business?"

"Who stirred the town up, anyway? It was Ledbetter and Breen, wasn't it—with maybe Dalhart to help. By the way, where is Dalhart?"

"He's dead. Your damned hunky killed him."

"Oh, no, he didn't. Joe didn't even fire his gun out there. If Dalhart's dead, it's you that killed him. But let that go for now. Haven't you ever wondered why those three hated Joe so much?"

Joe groped and found Molly's hand. She wasn't going to like this, and it was going to hurt.

Outside there was silence. Ed didn't need to shout now. "Let's take Dalhart first. He never did forgive Joe for the whipping Joe gave him that day in Rafferty's."

"What about Ledbetter?"

Joe's grip tightened on Molly's hand. Ed said loudly, "Ledbetter's quite a citizen, ain't he? Church member, banker, an' all?"

"Sure! Sure!" a man yelled. "But why does he hate Joe?"

"Remember Joe's mother? Sonja Redenko?"

A man snickered suggestively. "I'd like to have known her better. But I wasn't one of the lucky ones."

Joe flushed angrily in the darkness. Ed's voice also showed anger, for all its control. Ed said, "Ledbetter was. He visited Sonja every Saturday night. Joe caught him at it and told him to stay away."

Molly's indrawn breath startled Joe. She buried her face in his chest. "Oh, Joe, I'm sorry. I didn't know."

From the mob outside there were sounds of surprise, exclamations, and then, suddenly, loud, coarse laughter. Joe heard Ed sigh with relief. When a mob laughs, its teeth are dulled.

A man shouted, "Well, by God, I didn't think he had it in him!"

Ed gave them no time for discussion. "When Sonja was killed, Ledbetter turned to Susan Poole. And Joe was unlucky enough to catch him at that, too. Ledbetter let you all think he hated Joe on account of Molly, but that wasn't it at all."

A man whistled with amazement. Another snickered. Someone said, "No wonder Susan's always givin' him those moo-cow eyes."

There was a stirring on the floor, beside Joe's foot. He shoved Molly away from him quickly. "Get to the back wall of the cabin," he whispered, "and stay there. Don't make a sound, no matter what."

He wished he had a light. But he didn't. He knelt, and felt to see which one of the unconscious men had moved. His hand encountered Breen's bulky body, which was still. Ledbetter, then. Joe whispered, "Mr. Ledbetter, if you move, I'll have to slug you again."

He was conscious of a certain nervousness. He said, "Ed, Ledbetter's moving. Wish I could see him."

"Strike a match. It's all right now."

Joe did. He saw Ledbetter, fully conscious, crouched half a dozen feet away. He said sharply, "Damn it, stay where you are! Move and I'll shoot!"

The match died out, and Joe dropped it. The tension in Joe increased, because now he couldn't see Ledbetter at all. He couldn't see anything but the open doorway in which Ed stood.

Outside, someone yelled, "What about Breen?" in an expectant tone.

Another good sign. When a mob became interested in gossip and dirt, it lost its lust for blood.

Ed answered, "Breen fired Joe from his job at the store for stealing. But he suspected all along that it wasn't Joe at all, but his own boy, Willie. He knew Willie hated Joe, and suspected that Willie had planted the money on Joe."

"How come Breen would suspect Willie?"

Ed hesitated for a moment after that. When he spoke again it was with obvious reluctance. "Breen was an embezzler himself. He stole a couple of thousand from the people he worked for back East. He came out here and started his store with it. Later he got married. But he was always afraid, both of bein' caught and that Willie would end up bein' a thief too."

"Hell, if you knew all this, why the hell didn't you arrest Breen?"

"I didn't see any point in it. Breen was leading an honest life. I never did believe in holdin' a man's past mistakes against him all his life."

"How'd you find out about Breen?"

"A sheriff gets all kinds of 'Wanted' circulars."

There was utter silence outside the cabin now. Ed broke it, yelling, "Now get the hell out of here, all of you. Go on home. Maybe I'll be able to forget what's happened tonight, but I doubt it. Every damned one of you had better walk a narrow line from here on out!"

The men outside began to talk back and forth. The sounds blended into an uneasy murmur.

Joe held his breath. It didn't take much, he knew, to rouse a mob. It took a lot to stop one. But without the leaders who had roused them in the beginning . . . Well, it was a good chance.

They began to disperse. He heard someone shout, "Where's the horses?"

A long breath eased out of his lungs. He'd forgotten Ledbetter in the tension of the moment. Now he heard Ledbetter move, and warned Ed. "Look out!"

Ledbetter struck him like a charging steer. Joe was flung aside, falling. Ledbetter bowled Ed aside the same way and went out through the door.

Ed lay still, unmoving, just to one side of the door, visible only as a huddled form. Joe said sharply, "Molly, look after Ed." Then he flung himself through the door toward the retreating shape of Ledbetter.

Ledbetter stopped. He screamed irrationally, "Come back! Come back here, all of you! You going to ride off an' let that killer go?"

There wasn't much light, but Joe could see Ledbetter standing, legs spread, shaking his fist at the unseen posse members out in the darkness. Ledbetter must have snatched a rifle from Ed as he went through the door, for he held one now in his hand.

Out in the darkness, someone laughed. Another called an obscene jest at Ledbetter, one that concerned Sonja Redenko and Susan Poole.

Someone else shouted that down. "Hey! Shut up! We listened to Ed Mallory. Let's see what Roscoe's got to say."

All that Ed had done could be ruined in a few seconds by Ledbetter's eloquence.

Joe said, "I'm right here, Mr. Ledbetter. I'm not runnin' away."

He saw Ledbetter start with surprise. He saw Ledbetter whirl. Flame shot from the rifle's muzzle, once, twice.

Joe's own gun was in his hand. But he couldn't shoot. He couldn't stand here and kill Molly's father. But, if he could enrage Ledbetter enough to empty his rifle . . .

He said, "I'm not running away, but I'm going away. And I'm taking Molly with me. She's inside the cabin waiting right now."

The rifle roared again. Then the hammer came down on an empty chamber. Joe said, "All right, Mr. Ledbetter. Your rifle's empty. Throw it away and come on in the cabin if you want to tell Molly good-by."

He tried to make his voice sound friendly and respectful, the way a man ordinarily would with his prospective father-in-law, but it must have come out differently, for it only seemed to enrage Ledbetter more. Joe caught his movement an instant too late, and tried to swing away.

Ledbetter came at him like a bull, using the rifle as a club. Its stock swung viciously, close enough to Joe's head to knock his hat off.

Joe leaped back, off balance. Before him, dimly seen in the faint light, Ledbetter was half turned around by the momentum of the swinging rifle.

Suddenly there was light. Molly came running from the cabin door, carrying a battered, rusty, but lighted lantern. And behind her came Ed, staggering.

Joe's gun was still in his hand. But he didn't move. He couldn't. In the flickering lantern's light, he stared at Ledbetter, remembering all the old hatred and wondering where it had gone. Ledbetter had persecuted him since he'd been a child. He ought to hate Ledbetter more than anything on earth. But he didn't. He didn't hate him at all any more. And he knew he couldn't shoot him, or even fight back.

He was sick of fighting, sick of hurting and being hurt. It had to stop somewhere, and that somewhere was here.

Ledbetter recovered and drew the rifle back for another swing. He advanced toward Joe, powerful as a grizzly. His eyes were red and bloodshot, narrowed with insane fury. Something within Joe cringed, because what he saw in Ledbetter's eyes was madness.

Joe leaped back, ducking, and again the rifle stock whistled past, inches from his face.

Joe was sweating now, wearied from the day of tension and fear. His knees began to shake. One misstep now— That rifle stock could be more deadly than a bullet.

So far there had been no sound from Molly, and Joe dared not take his eyes from Ledbetter's face.

Perhaps he could have escaped in flight. But he would no

more flee from Ledbetter than he would fight him.

Ed Mallory was coming, and Joe knew he'd try to help if he had time—and enough strength.

He leaped away again as the rifle swung. Then Ledbetter began to curse. Words that were incredibly foul bubbled from his drooling mouth.

Joe realized that he was yelling, "Shut up! Shut up, damn you! You want Molly to hear that stuff?"

Ledbetter stopped. For an instant he was motionless, staring at Joe stupidly, as though he had not understood.

Ed was ready, for all his unsteadiness. He didn't let the opportunity pass. He stepped from the side of Joe's vision and brought his gun barrel down with exactly calculated force upon the top of Ledbetter's skull.

Ledbetter sagged. Ed caught him and eased him to the ground. Molly stared at her father for a moment, then ran and flung herself into Joe's arms. She was sobbing hysterically. "Joe, is that my own father? Is it really him?"

Ed said, "Get her away from here. Take my horse and hers." He raised his head and looked around at the gathered faces of the subdued lynchers who had been watching the fight. He said curtly, in command of the situation at last, "Don't stand there gawking. Dalhart's dead out in back of the cabin. Breen's inside. Load them on their horses and get started back to town. Breen I want in jail. The rest of you go home and wait till you hear from me."

"How about Joe? You bringin' him in?"

Ed's eyes blazed. "And give you another chance to pull what you pulled today? Not on your life. I'll have the coroner call some of you for Willie's inquest. And you'd better bring in a verdict of justifiable homicide. Understand?" His tone and his words gave them to understand that this was an ultimatum, not a request.

Silently they dispersed. A couple of them helped Breen, staggering, from the cabin. A couple more went after Dalhart's body. And after a while they were gone, riding quietly away through the timber.

Suddenly all the strength seemed to go out of Joe's legs. He looked at Ed and grinned shakily. "Ed, that was close." He unbuckled his gun and handed it to Ed. "If a man doesn't carry one, he ain't likely to use it. I decided that once before and then changed my mind. Shouldn't have."

He went to the edge of the clearing, where Molly's horse stood, munching grass. He picked up the reins, led the horse back. He lifted Molly to the saddle and mounted behind her. He said, smiling faintly, "Keep your horse, Ed. This one will do for us. There'll be no one on my trail any more."

For an instant he sat there, looking down, remembering the good things now and forgetting the bad. "You ask in Casper, Ed, where Dell Robineau's place is. You come see us when you can."

He hesitated for a moment more. He'd never been good at saying thanks. "Ed, I . . ."

Ed grinned. "Shut up and get out of here. A man don't have to say every damned thing he thinks, does he?"

Molly was smiling too. "He'd better—to me, anyway."

Joe pointed the horse north and rode away.

———

Ed sat down and trimmed the wick of the ancient, battered lantern. He was suddenly tired—tireder than he'd ever been in his life before.

Joe was gone. But Ed knew he'd always remember that last look he'd seen in Joe's eyes. It was plentiful payment for all that had happened—all the thanks Ed wanted. For it told him that Joe was at last at the reins of his own destiny. Joe, not circumstances, was in the driver's seat.

Center Point Publishing
600 Brooks Road • PO Box 1
Thorndike ME 04986-0001 USA

(207) 568-3717

US & Canada:
1 800 929-9108